Eulalia,
I hope you
enjoy the
story enclosed.
Love,
Lori

Published by Warren Publishing, Inc.
Huntersville, NC
www.warrenpublishing.net

ISBN: 978-0-9894814-96

Library of Congress Control Number: 2013943192

This book is lovingly dedicated to the memory of my father, Revis Crecelius, and to my mother, Janet Crecelius Johnson.

For Haden, Hadley, and Gibson~Mammie's little angels.

To my husband, Doug. Thank you for your love and support in everything that I do. I'm blessed beyond measure.

With love, to Jerry and Kathleen Roberts.

Special thanks and gratitude to Kathie Hicks Fuston.

Robert Barrow Sweeney: Thank you for your kindness and true Southern hospitality. Your memories and pictures of the home which your ancestors built and in which you grew up were priceless.

Charlotte Hopps~Another one of God's blessings in my life.

Prologue

COLUMBIA, TENNESSEE, 1925

The 1921 Dixie Flyer made its way up the narrow street, pulling over to the curb. The oriental green paint looked stark in contrast to the gray overcast that blanketed the quiet autumn day. Having come around the side to open the door, the driver stood waiting while a young girl dressed fashionably in a brown suit and hat extended her hand to the elderly woman still inside.

"Grandmother, do you want me to go on ahead and ring the bell?" her granddaughter inquired.

The aged one spoke softly, sounding as if her breath had all but left her.

"No, dear, there's no one here that would remember me now."

Standing on wobbling knees, she surveyed the long brick sidewalk that led to the large two-story brick home before her.

The young girl held on to her grandmother's withered hand, steadying her, as she approvingly eyed the stately home standing proudly before them. The memory of a time long ago brought a smile to the wrinkled face, letting a special light emit from the sagging folds of skin that all but veiled her eyes.

"Who lived here, Grandmother?" the girl asked.

Cordelia turned to her granddaughter, remembering an image only she could see.

"Love lived here."

GALLATIN, TENNESSEE, 1844

Lucretia Barlow knew this birth would be different from her last, only fifteen months before. Her pains had begun earlier that day, but she had delayed summoning her sister and Mammy Nancy from the adjoining room. It had been a difficult pregnancy for Lucretia, and that was the reason her sister had come from her home south of Nashville to tend her during her time of confinement.

Judge Barlow, almost twelve years his wife's senior, was away with a court case in nearby Goodlettsville when the birth pains began. He had been cold, barely giving his wife a passing glance since her condition was obvious. The small toddler lying asleep in the nursery down the hall received only slightly more affection than her mother.

Cordelia Barlow was a healthy, robust toddler. Her dark curls and large eyes reminded Lucretia Barlow of her own mother. Barely walking, she was allowed to see her mother only for a short time before the young Priscilla, servant to Lucretia, took the young child from her mother's birthing room.

JULY 1853

The incessant buzzing of the gnats circling Pharaoh's ear did little to improve his disposition as he walked along the well-worn path the slaves had made over the years at Fairview Plantation. As long as he could recollect, he had lived in one of the cabins amongst the row of white clapboard dwellings behind the big house of Judge Absalom Barlow. Pharaoh had been born at Dryer Hall, the tobacco and cotton plantation of Judge Barlow's first wife, Lucretia Dryer. If he had to guess, his people had been the Dryer's property since they were snatched over from de Guinea in Africa. Dr. Dryer had named him Pharaoh, said he had a look to him like the pictures of them fancy drawings on the tombs in Egypt. Pharaoh had no use for such things in the cotton fields of Tennessee. As far as he could see, he was more like the slaves old Pharaoh was lawdin' over.

Today, he was one of the fifteen fieldhands that had been working Judge Barlow's cotton field. It was going to be a good crop, thanks to the long hours he and the others had put into the field this spring. The afternoon sun was beginning to slouch down behind the big house. From the field, Pharaoh could see his wife, Cilla, short for Priscilla, toting the basket of sweet corn atop her turbaned head. She was a right handsome woman, thought Pharaoh, as he surveyed her hips swaying to and fro as she trudged up the dirt path to their cabin door. Pharaoh had been with Cilla since he was seventeen and she was sixteen. Dr. Dryer even said the marryin' words over them to make it as legal as it could be in slave times. The two came with Lucretia Dryer Barlow when she brought her slaves with her to Fairview. In no time, Priscilla became the mother of four youngins. All the memory that Pharaoh could recollect was slave times, and he wished for something better for his own youngins. For now, this was the long and short of his life: working from "can to can't," from when the sun stands up until it lays down in the night. Most of the slaves on the Barlow plantation had been with the judge since he married Lucretia Dryer. A total of 25 slaves now made up the Barlow slave family.

Life was such as this for all of Judge Barlow's servants, as he called them. Most would say he wasn't a cruel master; he provided for his people and didn't see benefit in a servant that was too sick or underfed to work. They had plenty to eat, and the judge made sure clothes were allotted to his people regularly. His overseer, Lucas Crenshaw, was the devil in breeches, so the black folks said. He would take the whip to a lazy darkie quicker than you could shake a stick. He wasn't above more severe punishment either, if he deemed it necessary. Judge Barlow left much of the plantation doings to Lucas. As of late, he was busy keeping company with a widowed socialite in town.

The big house, a large two-story dwelling with large Corinthian columns and a wide front porch, was left to his older, spinster sister to manage. Aunt Eugenie was beyond the age of managing a large plantation. Six years ago she had been summoned to Fairview when Judge Barlow's wife, Lucretia, had passed away giving birth to a lifeless son. Absalom Barlow knew nothing about raising children; the thought of being the sole caregiver to a one-year-old girl was something he feared more than a slave uprising.

Seven-year-old Cordelia Barlow spent this afternoon lying on the cool wooden floor of Mammy Cilla's cabin. If Aunt Eugenie caught wind of this favorite pastime, a litany of reprimands, as well as the sharp sting of a mulberry switch across her backside, would follow. Aunt Eugenie didn't mind Mammy Cilla having the love of Cordelia, but she wouldn't abide her young charge behaving like one of the servants. As far as Cordelia was concerned, what Aunt Eugenie didn't know wouldn't hurt her. She would steal away to the loving arms of Mammy Cilla whenever she could. The small cabin offered a haven for Cordelia, and the children of Cilla and Pharaoh were her playmates as she grew up at Fairview.

Mammy Cilla's cabin was a far cry from the finery that Cordelia was accustomed to at the big house. The only table was handmade by Pharaoh, and the few pieces of furniture to be seen in the sparsely decorated room were two high-back wooden chairs and a couple of small benches that Pharaoh had constructed years ago to accommodate his growing family. Next to the fireplace sat the small wooden rocking chair. This was passed down to Pharaoh from his Mammy. But it was the bed in the corner that Cordelia loved. Mammy Cilla wouldn't allow any of the darkie children to touch her quilted bed. However, she allowed Cordelia to find solace on the rope bed, between the soft sheets, when she was feeling poorly from eating too many pokeberries. The quilt was Cilla's most prized possession, made from the scraps of dresses that Cilla had saved as Aunt Eugenie tired of this bodice or that skirt. All of Judge Barlow's people knew she was the favorite of the mistress of Fairview.

"Aunt Eugenie, why does Father stay gone so long?" Cordelia asked, turning her small, round face toward the direction of her aunt. Putting her embroidery hoop aside, Eugenia fixed her gaze on Cordelia, her best smile showing.

"Cordelia, your papa has a good many cases to hear in and around these parts. You mustn't worry yourself about his being away," Eugenia replied. "Don't you remember him telling us about stopping off in Nashville to bring your new mother home to Fairview?"

Cordelia remembered her father telling her about Mrs. Marshall. She remembered how much she wanted to spend the afternoon that day with her father, lying on the large sofa in his study while he worked busily on matters of the court. She hadn't given this woman who would be her new mother much more than a passing thought.

"Do you think my new mother likes little girls?" Cordelia pondered, feeling a sense of dread snake itself around her insides.

As she made the comment, she made large circles with her tiny satin slipper thrust into the air. Aunt Eugenia saw her unladylike maneuver, and quickly made her way to the settee where her niece was lying. Hearing the movement of her aunt's taffeta skirt swishing about, Cordelia quickly sat upright.

Aunt Eugenie knew nothing of the new mistress of Fairview, but reached down to pat the young child on top of her curly head.

"Now don't you go fretting about such things, Cordie. You run along and find something to do. I need to speak with Mr. Crenshaw."

Satisfied with the reassurance from Aunt Eugenie, Cordelia skipped out the massive oak door, down the shaded brick walk that led past the summer kitchen, to the only person whose loving arms made everything seem better. If only Father could hug her like Mammy Cilla, or just tell her that he loved her best.

The sun was high in the sky, stretching its rays onto the row of tin roofs that covered the wood clapboard cabins of Judge Barlow's slaves. Cordelia listened to the chatter of the slave children behind Mammy Cilla's cabin. Benny and Silas sat cross-legged, rolling a ball of yarn back and forth in the dirt, while Matilda and Liza Ann played with their corn husk dolls, not hearing Cordelia's silent approach.

"Daddy say old massa fetchin' a new mama fo' miz Cordie," Matilda remarked, walking her doll across the dusty ground.

Liza Ann's gaze never lifted as she replied, "I heerd Mammy say old Miss gonna have her nose plumb outta joint on account of it."

Cordelia crouched low and crawled under the honeysuckle vines that coiled themselves around the old well pump and splitrail fence. The damp ground felt cool on her bare legs, and the smell of the dank soil somehow felt oddly welcoming.

The harvest time would soon be coming on, and Fairview was much like all the other plantations and farms in and around Gallatin, Tennessee. The overseers made use of optimum daylight during the months of July and August to get the crops in from the fields. Crenshaw became unusually cruel and showed little tolerance for a slave who was sick or lazy.

Judge Barlow had paid a hefty sum for Doc Lewis to make a call out to the slave cabins. It seemed the illness that started with one soon spread throughout the little row of cabins behind the big house. Aunt Eugenie tried to doctor the symptoms as best she knew how, but when it was decided this was beyond her care, Judge Barlow sent for the doctor. He had already seen his fields practically neglected, save for a few of the older slaves plodding away during the two-week illness that invaded his servant family.

Cordelia wasn't allowed to venture beyond the back of the house for fear of catching the flux that spread throughout the cabins. Mammy Cilla and Pharaoh came through it with only a few days of the fever and violent spasms that kept them weak as kittens. It was their youngest, Benny, who couldn't seem to gather his strength. The old doctor told them the typhoid fever had taken its hold, and little Benny would slip into eternal slumber that very evening.

Cordelia had never seen Pharaoh or Mammy Cilla cry before. The grievous sounds wafting up to the big house from the slave cabins frightened her. The thought of Mammy Cilla leaving her suddenly made

Benny's dying more painful to her. Death wasn't something she really knew much about, only that it was just like going to sleep and not waking up. She remembered her mother being very sleepy, then she was laid out in a big box downstairs in the parlor. She couldn't remember the babe who died before taking a breath. Now she began to think about Benny lying in the pine box in Pharaoh's cabin.

Aunt Eugenie wouldn't allow her to go along to pay respects for fear she would contract the flux. Cordelia waited until her aunt retired for the night. Creeping down the carpeted stairway, her satin slippers kept her secret as she made her way out the heavy door which led to the slave cabins.

Mammy Cilla was laying over Benny's coffin, weeping and wiping her tears on a long piece of cloth. Cordelia could see her through the window, the candle's flickering light casting her shadow on the wall behind her. She knew Aunt Eugenie would switch her good if she caught the flux, but her love for Mammy Cilla was far greater than her fear of punishment.

"Mammy, please don't cry," Cordelia said softly, startling Mammy Cilla from her moment of grief. "For Lawd, chile, what you be doin' here all by yoself?" Mammy Cilla said, rising from her chair. Hearing her, Pharaoh looked up from his vigil beside the child.

Cordelia ran to Mammy Cilla and put her little arms tightly around her soft waist.

"Mammy, please don't cry," Cordelia said softly. Cilla took the child and sat her on her lap.

"Miz Cordelia, you ain't suppose to be down here. Miz Eugenia be whipping the hide clean off yo' backside. Now run on, Mammy and Pharaoh just be sad cause Benny ain't gonna be with us no mo'."

Cordelia could see the feet of little Benny down in the coffin from her perch on Mammy Cilla's lap.

"You wanna see him, miz Cordelia?" Pharaoh asked. He knew her just being in the cabin could bring about a severe whipping by the overseer if he caught wind of her being there.

Cordelia nodded her head, then peered down into the box where the little boy lay peacefully.

"He don't look sick, Mammy," Cordelia said, almost disbelieving that he was dead.

Cilla began to weep again, and Pharaoh bent down to touch the young boy's curly head.

"He be sleepin', Miz Cordie. Already gone to the Lawd where he be free and no mo' bein' a slave."

Pharaoh wiped his eyes as a steady stream of tears flowed down his ebony cheeks. Cordelia then noticed the other slaves who were sitting in the little room. They began to sing a mournful song, and they gathered around the coffin, swaying and wiping their tears singing, "Oh Mary, Don't Ya Weep, Don't Ya Mourn." Cordelia wanted Mammy Cilla to stop crying, to be happy again. She wondered if Benny was in Heaven with her mama.

The next day, the slaves were allowed to break from their labors to bury the young child and mourn the death of another on the plantation. Cordelia watched from her bedroom window as her father touched Mammy Cilla's shoulder sympathetically, saying words over Benny's little mound of dirt. He didn't even come to check on her, going out to the slave cemetery first. In her father's room at the end of the hall was her new mother, Rachel. Sometime earlier the evening before, her father brought his new wife and her servants to live at Fairview.

After breakfast, Rachel Barlow descended the stairway into the formal parlor. Cordelia was lying on the couch, listening to her father and Lucas Crenshaw discussing slave issues occurring during Absalom's absence over the last three weeks. When Rachel cleared her throat rather loudly, the two men suspended their conversation.

"Mr. Crenshaw, this is my wife, Mrs. Barlow," Absalom said, smiling at her.

Lucas Crenshaw smiled, tipping his cap. He looked the new mistress of Fairview over, imagining her shapely form without her chemise and drawers. His eyes darted toward the floor, almost giving away his adulterous thoughts.

"Pleased to meet you, Mrs. Barlow. You won't have to be worrying yourself over the Negras on this plantation. I have a firm hand over them."

Absalom Barlow didn't like the tone his overseer used in regard to his servants.

"Yes, well, that will be all for today, Mr. Crenshaw. I would like to take Mrs. Barlow around the grounds to show her Fairview properly," Judge Barlow countered.

Cordelia was invisible to the adults in the room. She moved from her place on the couch, and it was then that Rachel saw her.

"Who do we have here?" Rachel asked, using what she thought was her best motherly tone.

Cordelia slowly walked over to her new stepmother, noticing the smell of rose water as she came closer. She had to stretch her neck to look at Rachel Barlow's dark black eyes.

"Cordelia, please introduce yourself properly to your new mother," her father reprimanded.

Cordelia's throat suddenly felt dry; she wasn't sure why the cat suddenly caught her tongue.

"My name is Cordelia Lucretia Barlow, and I'm nine years old."

The judge smiled at his new wife as Cordelia made her formal introductions. Rachel bent down to set her eyes evenly with her stepdaughter's.

"I'm very pleased to meet you Cordelia. I hope you are a good girl, not like those Negro children you have been playing with for so long."

With that comment, she turned to her husband, her tone changing as she spoke.

"Absalom, you must put a stop to her being down in the slave quarters like a common pickaninny. A young lady should be spending her time at the academy, learning the proper social graces," Rachel implored.

Cordelia felt her new mother's comments were meant to be something bad, as if she were not to be friends with Pharaoh and Mammy Cilla's children, or even the other slaves' children that were her playmates.

Absalom had given full reign in the rearing of his daughter to his sister, Eugenia. Since the passing of his wife, Lucretia, he had kept himself busy with traveling back and forth to Nashville. He wasn't a very affectionate man, barely giving Cordelia a hug or kiss. He also never spoke of his wife. Cordelia wondered if Father cried for her mother and the baby lying beneath the blanket of grass as Pharaoh and Mammy Cilla cried for Benny.

That evening, Cordelia thought about Benny's little form lying all alone in the wooden box in Mammy Cilla's cabin. She couldn't remember her mother or the baby. She tried to fall asleep thinking about pleasant things as Aunt Eugenie would tell her when she began to worry and fret over something. The one thought that brought such peace to her little soul was Mammy Cilla and her loving arms.

Eugenia sent for Lucas Crenshaw. She had overheard Spicey and Nancy talking about the whipping he had given to two slaves. The two had been relieved of their afternoon duties due to the flux they had contracted. Lucas had whipped them both for lying down on the carpet of grass under the willow tree down by the spring.

Lucas made his way up to the large doors of Fairview. He stood, waiting before he knocked. He adjusted the cap squarely on his head, then rapped the door rather loudly. Spicey opened the door slowly, seeing it was devil Crenshaw.

"Afternoon, Mr. Crenshaw. Miz Eugenia said to go on to the parlor, she waitin' for you in there," Spicey said, not wanting to look him in the eye.

"Move out of my way, girl. I know where the parlor is," Lucas snapped.

He made his way down the hallway, taking his cap off before entering the formal parlor.

"Come in, Mr. Crenshaw. I would like to speak to you," Eugenia commanded. "Mr. Crenshaw, I won't bother dancing around the purpose of my summoning you. I was told of a beating Thursday last, one which you had no right to give."

Lucas felt the tide of anger rising. He couldn't abide the likes of any woman questioning his authority in the overseeing of Fairview.

"Now Miss Eugenia, there's no sense in getting all riled over two lazy darkies. The judge himself left the discipline to me where his Negras are concerned, Ma'am. They deserved that whippin', and I was just doin' what the judge wanted."

Eugenia moved from her place on the settee, coming within inches of Lucas Crenshaw's face. "Billy and Josiah had been down with the flux. You had no right. I will be speaking to my brother about this. And another thing, Mr. Crenshaw. You are to stay away from Molly's cabin. Do I make myself perfectly clear?" Eugenia snapped.

The last words took Lucas by surprise. He was sure he and the young slave had kept their meetings a secret from the Barlows. This was one thing the judge would not abide ~ his overseer taking liberties with his slaves.

"I don't know what you mean, Miss Eugenia," Lucas lied.

"I'm sure that you do, and I will be speaking to my brother about you. Perhaps Fairview needs a new overseer," Eugenia said, seeing the look of disdain in his eyes.

"Is that all you wanted to talk to me about?" Lucas asked, suddenly wanting to be out of the presence of Eugenia Barlow.

"Yes, you may go. But remember, you are just an employee of the Barlow family, Mr. Crenshaw."

Lucas made his way out of the room, almost knocking the tray out of Nancy's hands as he moved past her on the way out the front door.

"'Scuze me, Mr. Crenshaw," Nancy said, smiling at the conversation she had overheard.

Nancy and the other slaves knew Lucas Crenshaw was the father of that baby Molly was going to be bringing into the world, even if the judge didn't know of it yet. Secrets were something the slaves were accustomed to at Fairview. They had kept a few over the years, and they weren't alone in harboring secrets on this plantation.

Eugenia didn't like Mr. Crenshaw, and since arriving six years ago, always felt an uneasiness when near him. She wondered why her brother would dismiss the more amiable Benton Hallert, the previous overseer. There was only a slight mention of his name when she arrived. Something about him having to leave abruptly, but nothing more was said. What brought him to mind now puzzled Eugenia, but she let the thought pass. She walked out of the parlor, just as Nancy entered with her tea.

"Nancy, if you don't mind, I'm not going to be needing my tea just now. Please take it back to the kitchen."

Nancy knew the conversation with old devil Crenshaw had left her in a mood. She moved to let Eugenia pass.

"Yes'm, Miz Eugenia. I'll be takin' this back to da kitchen."

Eugenia made her way down the hallway to the large stairway. As she started up the steps, she noticed Crenshaw glaring back at the house before mounting his horse. She continued up the stairs, remembering her mission at hand. Just as she was about to knock on the bedroom door, she overheard her brother and his new wife speaking softly.

"I would be happy to write the proper inquiries to locate the perfect academy in Nashville for Cordelia," Rachel offered sweetly. "Of course, you know what is best for your daughter. I just don't see how fitting it is for a nine-year-old girl to be spending all her time with the slaves."

Absalom raked his long fingers through the thick mane that had begun to turn grey near his temples. He was twenty years beyond his new bride, priding himself on such a fine catch. He didn't much like Cordelia spending her time with the servants, but there were no finer darkies in all of Sumner County than Pharaoh and Mammy Cilla. Why, Pharaoh's own mother was Lucretia's nursemaid from birth. Perhaps that is why they were held in such high regard at Fairview. He didn't see how he could discourage Cordelia from spending time with them and their children. They had always been hardworking, loyal servants.

"Rachel, darling, my sister has done an exemplary job raising Cordelia in the way our own mother raised the two of us. I don't think sending Cordelia away from Fairview at this young age would be of benefit to her rearing," Absalom stated.

Mammy Cilla brought a large dressmaker's dummy down from the attic, Matilda toting a bolt of fabric that was obviously too heavy for her nine-year-old hands to manage. Aunt Eugenia had summoned Mammy Cilla early that morning to fetch the patterns and material for a special dress.

"Now don't you be draggin' Miz Eugenie's prized tafta 'cross da floor, girl. I ain't goin' ta' have Miz Eugenie wearin' yo' dirty footprints across dis here new dress," Mammy snapped.

Matilda tried to hoist the bolt of taffeta higher on her shoulder, trying her best not to trip over the heavy material.

"Yas'm, Mammy," Matilda softly replied.

Cordelia heard the commotion outside her bedroom. The rustle of Mammy Cilla's skirts meant she would be downstairs before Cordelia could don her slippers and wrap.

Aunt Eugenia was bent over the dress patterns trying to find a suitable gown for traveling. It had been quite some time since she had taken leave of the plantation, and whenever she did, a new frock was in order. Mammy Cilla had been making the dresses for Eugenia Barlow since she arrived at Fairview. She was about to make another on this fine fall day.

Mammy Cilla and Aunt Eugenia began arranging the fabric on the large rosewood dining room table. Cordelia entered the dining room unnoticed, crawling under the table to sit with Matilda.

"Wanna go outside and play with the new doll Father brought me?" Cordelia whispered, leaning into Matilda's ear.

Since Matilda had no real dolls to play with, the offer didn't need to be in the form of a question. Matilda had already scooted herself from beneath the table, making sure she didn't catch the drooping end of the linen tablecloth as she left her hiding spot. She almost made it past the keen ears of Mammy Cilla. Cordelia slipped back under the table.

"What you be sneakin' around de floor, Tillie?" Mammy questioned, giving Matilda a look.

"Mammy, Miz Cordie wonts me ta play wit her new dollbaby," Matilda said in a simpering manner.

It was then Cordelia came out from her hiding place, sensing she needed to come to her friend's aid. Looking up from her dress patterns, Aunt Eugenia turned to Cordelia.

"I don't see what harm it would be for you to take Matilda outside. You girls will just be underfoot while we are cutting the pattern," she announced.

Cilla felt something was bothering her mistress; she had been very quiet as of late.

"Miz Eugenia, I's sorry for mah girl bein' in da way. She has chores down in da' garden."

Mammy turned and gave Matilda a look again. Few words needed to be exchanged between the two. It was something they had been taught: obedience to the Master without question. Mammy Cilla had never questioned her lot. She had been loyal to Judge Barlow's first wife, Lucretia, and felt her mistress would come back as a haunt if she let anything happen to her little girl. Maybe that was the reason Mammy Cilla showered Cordelia with the love the Master had denied her and her mother. It was something Eugenia Barlow didn't like, but she herself had no idea how to show the affection she so desperately needed. Cordelia frowned as her playmate was sent to the garden, leaving her once again alone in the quiet house. She took her new doll and walked sullenly to her room.

Since her arrival at Fairview, Rachel Barlow had found little about plantation life that interested her. Her days had been filled with making sure there was plenty of brandy in the glass decanter in the judge's study, and discussing with Spicey, the cook, what foods she would be preparing for the meal that day. She quickly saw that Absalom Barlow was a man of means, and his successes in the courts had afforded him quite a comfortable lifestyle. The furniture wasn't as fine as she expected someone of his means to have, but the home was furnished with family heirlooms that attracted her eye. Hanging above the mantle in the formal parlor was a sword from the Revolutionary War. She was too short to see the inscription on the sheath. Perhaps the judge was the son of a decorated soldier.

Rachel Greely married Francis Marshall, an up-and-coming member of the Democratic Party in Nashville, when she was 21 and he was 30. Their residence was one of the loveliest new homes in Nashville, and frequent visits by local politicians kept the Marshalls in the public eye.

Rachel was widowed at a young age, the dashing Marshall mortally wounded in a carriage accident on his way home from a political meeting. She was left to manage a large home with several servants. Her eye quickly revolved around gentlemen again once her period of mourning passed.

Rachel met the much older Judge Absalom Barlow at the home of the Governor during the previous Christmas season. Besides being enamored with her piercing dark eyes, Barlow became captivated with her witty conversational skills. She found Absalom charming, but wasn't attracted to him. It was only after she weighed her options for her future, and the somewhat less-than-adequate estate her deceased husband had left her, that she began to see the older judge and widower in a new light.

Rachel watched her young stepdaughter, Cordelia, running across the front lawn of Fairview Plantation with two Negro children, her braids hanging loosely in her face and the front of her dress covered in dirt. She never expected to have a young child to raise when she first met Judge Barlow. He waited to mention his daughter, keeping her a well-kept secret, until several months into their courtship. Why he wasn't forthcoming in his fatherhood baffled Rachel, but she didn't let her impending motherhood cause her to back away from their relationship. Now, here she was, miles from society and balls, and the only female with whom she could carry on an intelligent conversation was twice her age, and not of interest to her. Eugenia Barlow didn't hold her new sister-in-law in any higher regard.

She sat staring now at this child with whom she was to be a mother, and didn't find the task appealing. Children were always underfoot, and this child needed proper schooling and grooming. That Cordelia spent more time in the slave cabins than in the plantation house had not missed the attention of her new mother.

"Cordelia, you need to fix your hair and change your dress for dinner," Rachel said from her perch on the front porch.

Cordelia stopped in her tracks, her two young slave charges practically knocking her down from her abrupt halt. Matilda and Liza Ann looked at their young miss' dress, noticing a small rip in the hem. Their patched dresses looked much worse than the little tear in Cordelia's. When Cordelia made her way up the steps to the big house, her appearance drew a sharp comment from the new Mrs. Barlow.

"Cordelia! Look at your new dress. March yourself upstairs this instant and clean yourself."

Cordelia wasn't used to having someone other than Aunt Eugenia reprimanding her. Granted, she was a sight, her braids now mostly long strands of wavy curls, and it appeared there was a remnant of corn silk stuck to one of the strands. Matilda and Liza Ann stood as still as the gravestones behind the slave cabins.

"You girls run on now. Go help Cilla and Pharaoh do their chores. You've done enough playing for one day," Rachel snapped.

Cordelia looked over her shoulder as her two playmates ran barefoot across the sloping backyard, down the path to the back of their cabin. Making tiny balls with her fists, Cordelia turned toward her new mother.

"I'm sorry, Mother. I didn't mean to ruin the dress," Cordelia said, seeking some sort of compassion, and swallowing hard to keep from crying.

Rachel stood, smoothing down her skirt. She placed her hand under the child's quivering chin.

"Cordelia, you are getting to be a young lady. How would you like to go to Nashville and be with other little girls your age?" Rachel asked, smiling.

Cordelia had never been to Nashville. She had heard her father and Aunt Eugenia mention that place many times. She just couldn't imagine being away from Mammy Cilla, though.

"You will like school, Cordelia. There are several fine academies for young ladies, and you can come home for visits on vacations."

Cordelia suddenly felt afraid. Why was her new mother wanting her to go to school? She had all the education she needed with Aunt Eugenia teaching her numbers and letters, and she even could read from the Primer on the bookshelf. Rachel surveyed Cordelia's face, looking for some interest in her offer.

"I don't want to go," Cordelia snapped.

She didn't like the thought of leaving Mammy Cilla and Aunt Eugenie. Cordelia walked past her new mother, up the massive stairway to her room. She took off her soiled dress, throwing it on the floor, and climbed onto her bed, hugging the doll that her father had brought from Nashville. Presently, she heard a knock on her door.

"Cordelia, its Aunt Eugenia. May I come in?"

Cordelia quickly picked up her dirt covered dress and opened the door. Eugenia, seeing the child's tear-stained face, immediately bent to hug her. The gesture surprised Cordelia.

"Cordelia, I wanted to talk to you. Come sit on the bed with me," Eugenia gentled as she took Cordelia's hand and led her to the bed.

Cordelia sat on the bed, waiting to hear what Eugenia wanted to say. For a moment, Eugenia sat collecting her thoughts, then spoke.

"Cordelia, I am going to be leaving Fairview. I am going to live with my sister, your aunt, in Chattanooga," Eugenia uttered abruptly.

Cordelia blinked once, not sure what to say.

"Did I do something bad?" Cordelia asked.

Eugenia quickly gave Cordelia another hug, something out of character.

"Land sakes, child! You have done nothing wrong. I'm no longer needed here now that you have a mother," Eugenia said, trying to sound matter of fact.

"Why do you have to go?" Cordelia asked, puzzled and upset by her aunt's announcement.

Eugenia smiled, then continued,

"Your Aunt Irene has been feeling poorly since her daughter, Louisa, passed from scarlet fever. She needs me to help with her other children until she is back to health," Eugenia said.

Cordelia barely remembered her cousin, Louisa, and couldn't remember a time when Aunt Eugenia wasn't at Fairview.

"When will you be back, Aunt Eugenie?" Cordelia asked in a shaky voice.

Eugenia, trying to keep her composure, found the words halting in her throat, making speech almost impossible.

"I won't, dear. I will be leaving at the end of the week."

Cordelia reached up and put her arms around her aunt's neck. She squeezed her arms tightly together, bringing Eugenia's face close to hers.

Eugenia wasn't used to such depth of emotion. Where the tears came from, she wasn't sure. Trying her best, she composed herself and continued,

"Cordie, I never had children of my own. I tried to do my best by you. But I'm not your mother. Your papa has brought a new mother for you, and she feels, well, it would be best if I went to help Irene now."

"Aunt Eugenie, please don't leave. I don't like Mother. She is mean and doesn't like Matilda and Liza," Cordelia blurted.

Eugenia tried to think of something kind to say about Rachel Barlow, but at the present, was bereft of words. The new mistress of Fairview had made her wishes known to her quite plainly. There was no need for the aged woman to stay on at Fairview now that she was there. Something about Rachel Barlow didn't set well with Eugenia. Whatever her motives for suggesting Eugenia find residence elsewhere, evidently Eugenia Barlow had overstayed her welcome.

"Cordelia, I have sent a letter to your Aunt Irene, telling her of my arrival at the end of the week. I'll tell your father when he returns from

Nashville tonight," Eugenia said, swallowing the lump that had risen in her throat.

Cordelia hugged her doll closer. "May I go down to Mammy's cabin?" Cordelia asked softly.

The question took Eugenia by surprise and, giving her permission with a shake of her head, she stood from her place on the bed. Apparently, the conversation was over between the child and herself.

The afternoon's labors over for the day, Judge Barlow's servant quarters was a place where Cordelia often wandered. Playing with the children of her father's slaves, Cordelia often saw and heard the African talk and customs not often displayed within the watchful eye of their master or his overseer. It was a more relaxed time for the slaves of Fairview. Cordelia walked between the two rows of cabins, their doors wide open to allow whatever breeze could flow through on this hot, sultry afternoon. Sitting under a large walnut tree, Mammy Cilla, Pharaoh, Old Thomas, Mammy Nancy, Spicey, and Mordachi were breaking beans into large reed baskets.

"He as lazy as old hound dog leanin' against the fence to bark," Old Thomas said, laughing before he could finish the sentence.

"Dat devil Crenshaw workin' us ol' darkies 'cause he such a big boss, only he be settin' his own store fo' the winter," Pharaoh added.

Mammy Cilla sat her empty bowl down, leaning in closer to Nancy.

"De judge don't knows everything goes on whilst he away. Ol' Lucas best be careful aroun' new Miss. He best be walkin' right."

Nancy knew the meaning of Cilla's words. The two had been privy to events when the first mistress of Fairview was alive. The slaves of Judge Barlow knew more about the goings on at Fairview than he. Many of the younger slaves were unaware of the earlier overseer and his sudden absence. The young Benton Hallert didn't know the judge was on to his secret, just like the judge didn't know the watchful eyes of Nancy and Cilla were privy to his.

Cordelia made her way over to where the group was sitting. When Mammy Cilla saw Cordelia, she raised her eyebrows.

"Miz Cordie, the youngins be down by the creek. They's tryin' out that new fishin' line Old Thomas made them."

Cordelia smiled, knowing that a trip down to the creek meant taking off the stiff shoes her stepmother expected her to wear.

"Yo sho' is lookin' mighty pretty, darlin'," Mammy Cilla said.

Nancy added, offering a stern word of advice," Miz Cordie, you be careful down in that crick. Ain't no good reason fo' you to be down there in yo' pretty dress."

Cordelia hugged Mammy Cilla, giving her a quick kiss on her cheek, not listening to the older admonitions of Nancy. She would rather stay and talk to Mammy, but the creek and her playmates' voices were a distraction that couldn't be avoided on this hot day. Off she ran over the hill to the sounds of children's carefree laughter.

"Crenshaw been hangin' round the big house after ol' Judge goes to town. Don't know what he think he be doin' actin' like a buck in the rut. Miz Rachel be too uppity fo' his likes," Pharaoh insinuated.

"I think she just plain mean. I heerd her tell old Miss she just be underfoot now, it time she move on from here," Mammy said, her voice lowered.

Spicey, who had been quiet up to this point, added, "Miss Eugenie be leavin' day after the morrow. I over heerd her tell Judge Barlow while I was servin' his dinner. She be leavin' to go to Chattanooga. Miz Rachel tell me to let her girl cook her food. I's not givin' up my kitchen to her girl no how."

All conversation halted as Lucas Crenshaw came riding up to the group, obviously in a demanding mood.

"Judge Barlow wants the lower field harvested by the week's end. You be out in the field before sunup tomorrow. Bring those worthless youngins out there, Pharaoh! We need them to carry tobacco back to the barn."

Pharaoh didn't let the bile rising in his throat stop him from answering, "Yass'r boss. We be out there befo' Mister Sun pulls up da shade."

Lucas wasn't amused with the answer. Smirking, he condescended, "That's a good boy, Pharaoh. Judge don't need no lazy Negras on this plantation. They go down river, remember that."

"Yass'r, boss, ol' Pharaoh knows."

Old Thomas spat the juice of his tobacco in a defiant manner, knowing the judge didn't expect him to work the fields any longer. He was his oldest slave, and came from Harpeth County with the judge upon his marriage to the first Mrs. Barlow.

The slaves continued their talk, only the subject matter took a different turn.

“You ‘spect ol’ Judge know’d that baby was Boss Hallert’s?” Thomas said, wiping the tobacco juice from his chin with his tattered sleeve.

Nancy looked at Cilla, her eyes widening, “I sho’ do thinks so, Thomas. I sho do!”

Cilla’s knowing glance didn’t escape Pharaoh’s eye. They had a secret, too.

Cordelia watched as her Aunt Eugenia hugged Mammy Cilla and Spicey. Nancy wiped her eyes, presenting Miss Eugenia with a basket of her warm biscuits.

"You need somethin' fo the road, Miz Eugenie. I sho' is goin' to miss you."

Eugenia was touched by the emotions of the women. She smiled at each, touching their hands in an unusually kind gesture.

"Spicey, you remember the judge likes his cornbread and honey just so," Eugenia reminded.

"Mammy Cilla, you will find a box of scraps in your cabin. I had Pharaoh carry it down for you."

Cilla was proud that Miss Eugenia remembered her with this fine gift.

"Oh, Miz Eugenie, thank you kindly," Cilla beamed.

Then, to Cilla, she gave a stern warning. "Be good and mind yourselves. Watch over the child. I know she loves you best."

Eugenia Barlow bid her goodbyes to each of the servants of Fairview that day. Her brother made his way down from the large porch to help his sister into the carriage.

"I wish you would change your mind, Eugenia. I'm sure Irene will get along just fine," Judge Barlow said, looking over to his wife, and finding her gone.

Eugenia smiled, patting her brother's leathery hand.

"Now, Absalom. We have talked about this day coming, and it is time. Rachel has things well under control, and in time, Cordelia will know her as Mother," Eugenia said.

"Where is Cordelia? I wanted to tell her goodbye," Eugenia said, looking through the crowd of slaves for her young niece.

It was then that she saw the black, squinty eyes of Lucas Crenshaw staring at her. He smiled, tipping his hat in an apparent gesture only she understood. Cordelia saw her aunt from her bedroom window. She wasn't sure why she chose to remain in her bedroom, but felt that the adults wouldn't notice her anyhow. Just then, the door to her bedroom opened, her stepmother walking inside.

"Cordelia, come along and say goodbye to your Aunt Eugenia. You shouldn't be so rude," Rachel Barlow said sternly.

Cordelia quickly walked behind her stepmother, suddenly feeling badly about her behavior. She saw the long faces of the servants who stood solemnly in the yard. She made her way down the stone steps to the yard where her aunt was waiting by the carriage. Judge Barlow walked over to his daughter, bending down to her level, saying, "You should be ashamed for making your Aunt Eugenia wait on you, Cordelia. Say your goodbyes, please."

Cordelia reached up to give her aunt a hug. She kissed her cheek, then without emotion, said, "Goodbye, Aunt Eugenia."

Eugenia climbed into the carriage. She smiled at Cordelia, saying," Goodbye, Cordelia. I'll miss you."

And that was Cordelia's last memory of her Aunt Eugenia. She would never see or hear from her again.

The weeks following the harvest time were much anticipated by the slaves and their children. It was a time when the slaves were out of the fields and doing the work around the plantation that was less backbreaking. It was also a time when the children were more carefree in their play. Cordelia, Matilda, and Liza Ann spent more of their time playing with their dolls, while Silas chose to play with the wooden animals Pharaoh and Old Thomas had carved. Although Cordelia wasn't allowed to bring her dolls outside, she played alongside the slave children with their handmade toys. The memories of this last summer together would remain etched in Cordelia's memory. She heard the songs the fieldhands were singing, and she found herself singing the same songs, until her stepmother heard her. It was her 10th birthday, and she would remember this as being one of the last happy times she had with her father's slaves at Fairview Plantation.

Cordelia folded the small doll quilt neatly into the trunk lying on the bedroom floor. This special gift would accompany her to the Nashville Female Academy, something to keep Mammy Cilla close to her. It was the gift Mammy Cilla made for her doll, Elizabeth, on her birthday weeks earlier.

Her stepmother had made all the school arrangements, something for which Absalom Barlow was thankful. He knew of the Nashville Female Academy, even rode in his carriage past it on many occasions, but he wasn't sure his daughter was ready for formal education. Since his sister had left Fairview, Cordelia's education had come to an abrupt halt. Maybe it was best for her to devote more time to a proper education, one that would make her more propitious in the eyes of a future suitor.

Cordelia left her task and walked downstairs. It seemed Rachel Barlow ran a tight ship. The house servants were busy dusting and polishing the tea service, while two young boys worked hard beating the rugs with a large metal paddle out on the front lawn. The rope that hung between the two tall elm trees could hold three of the large oriental rugs that lay on the parlor, dining room, and library floors at Fairview. Presently, Silas and Tucker took turns smacking the rugs. Rachel had the other slave children stuffing pillows with goose feathers on the porch. It seemed she always had a job for someone to do.

Cordelia walked past the children, seeing Mammy Cilla and her girls, Matilda and Liza Ann, walking with the laundry baskets balanced atop their heads.

"Mammy Cilla, will you help me pack my trunk? I don't want to ask Mother. She is busy," Cordelia said, unaware of how her request must have sounded to Cilla.

Matilda and Liza Ann were unaffected by their mistress' request. They continued on with the laundry inside the house as Cilla put her load down on the step.

"Miz Cordie, you know Mammy Cilla be happy to help. You leavin' is gonna be a sad day for me and ol' Pharaoh," Mammy Cilla said sadly.

She put her arms around Cordelia, pulling her close. Cordelia could smell the sweat rising from Mammy Cilla's dress. She had been working in the washhouse all morning, a task that was especially tiresome on this warm, fall day. It didn't offend her nostrils as she breathed in the smell. Mammy Cilla's affection was something she had known all her days, as far back as her memory would reach.

"Thank you, Mammy. Can you go with me to Nashville?" Cordelia asked.

As Cilla bent down to lift the laundry basket, she laughed at the thought. She could barely read, only a few words after her own name.

"No, Lamb. Mammy Cilla has to stay behind an' take care of Judge and ol' Pharaoh and Tillie, Liza and Silas.

You be comin' fo visits tho."

That night, Cordelia stayed for a long time in Pharaoh and Cilla's cabin. She loved listening to the slave songs coming from the cabins. She watched as Pharaoh and Mammy Cilla held their children, giving them kisses before they went to sleep on their pallets. This night, she lay atop the rope bed of Mammy Cilla and Pharaoh. She was almost asleep when her stepmother appeared at the open door of the cabin.

"Cordelia, you need to get up to the house right now. Your father is home and wants to see you before you leave tomorrow."

Pharaoh and Mammy Cilla each bent down to hug Cordelia. She kissed each on their cheeks, bidding them a good night. The slaves began coming out of their cabins upon hearing the shrill voice of the mistress of Fairview. The sounds of their 'good nights' to Cordelia faded as the two walked up the path to the big house.

Lying in her large canopy bed, she felt a wave of melancholy overtake her as she tried to remember her father ever tucking her in. She never remembered a mother singing songs to her, only Aunt Eugenia telling her pleasant dreams before she walked up to her bed alone.

The moonlight coming through the window that evening cast an eerie shadow on the wall in Cordelia's room. She tried to will the scary thoughts away, but couldn't shake the feeling that began to coil in the pit of her stomach. She remembered hearing the stories from the slave quarters, of spirits coming back as a haunt. Old Thomas and Nancy talked of the conjures that were done by the older slaves at Fairview. She wondered if her mother ever came back as a haunt. On this night, she thought a lot about her mother. There was only one portrait in the house of Lucretia Barlow. The painting, done when she was a young woman and the new mistress of Fairview, hung from the same wall as when Old Thomas put the nail squarely in place.

Cordelia would often stand and study the portrait of her mother, trying to see if the picture would talk to her. As long as she could remember, her mother never came to visit her while she slept or when she was awake. She suddenly missed having her mother, and she didn't want to leave Mammy Cilla.

She donned her slippers and wrap, quietly descending the wide stairway that led to the large entry hall that welcomed visitors and friends alike into the large house. She crept into the moonlit parlor. Striking a match and lighting the table candle, she moved as silently across the room as a prowler, walking toward her mother's portrait. Staring up at the beautiful oil painting hanging from golden threads, Cordelia studied the small, round face. Her mother looked like a kind woman, someone Cordelia wished she could have known. Mammy Cilla had told her very little about her mother, only that she sat with her when she went with the angels to Heaven. Cordelia felt Mammy Cilla was the closest thing she had to her mother. Satisfied that her mother did go to Heaven, she smiled at the portrait and walked quietly back to her bed. For the rest of that night, her last night at Fairview, Cordelia Barlow dreamed the most pleasant dreams.

The following morning, Mammy Cilla brought her a breakfast tray so that she could have her breakfast in her room. After carefully placing the tray on the bedside table, she sat on the bed beside Cordelia.

"Good morning, Mammy," Cordelia said, rubbing her eyes with the back of her hand.

Cilla reached out to hold the hand of the child she loved as her own. "Miz Cordie, Pharaoh and me wants to give you somethin' ta' take with you to your schoolin'. It ain't much, no how," Cilla said, reaching into the pocket of her apron.

She handed Cordelia a small object wrapped in a piece of material. Cordelia took the gift, looking back at Mammy Cilla, smiling. She always loved presents.

"Thank you, Mammy! What is it?" Cordelia excitedly inquired.

"Open it, Miz Cordie!" Mammy said, anxious to see her expression when the gift was unwrapped.

Cordelia slowly opened her gift, careful not to drop the contents. There, in the fold of material, was an angel, its wings spread out like the dove that had built its nest in the magnolia tree outside her bedroom window. The angel had been carved lovingly from a block of wood with soft, delicate features. The work of Pharaoh obviously pleased the child very much. Cordelia turned the work of art over in her hands, examining the details of the robe.

"Pharaoh started on it back befo' your birthday, Miz Cordie. He sho' is proud of how she turned out," Cilla beamed, waiting for Cordelia to respond.

"She's the most beautiful thing I have ever seen, Mammy. Thank you! She reminds me of Mother."

Mammy Cilla smiled, proud that Cordelia could see a resemblance to the portrait in the parlor.

"Yes'm, Miz Cordie, he was trying to make her look like how we remember yo' mama. Now she can go with ya' ta' the acad'my."

Cordelia hugged Mammy Cilla tightly, breathing in the smell of her. Mammy Cilla felt the warm trickle of tears dropping on her neck as she pulled Cordelia tighter.

"Chile, you is just like ma' own. Me and Pharaoh sho' is gonna miss you, Lamb," Mammy said, rising from the bed.

Mammy Cilla took the empty tray and left Cordelia to finish her breakfast. Later that morning, she would be leaving the plantation for her new home and school several hours away in Nashville.

Cordelia came down the stairs like a condemned prisoner being led to the gallows. Silas, Matilda and Liza Ann walked beside her, sad that their playmate would be leaving. Pharaoh, Nancy, and Old Thomas were busy loading her trunks in the wagon. The leaves on the elm trees had begun to turn slightly, a covering of bright shades of orange and yellow. The pumpkins and gourds would soon be ready, and the vines that snaked around the smokehouse were loaded with this year's harvest. Cordelia noticed every detail as she walked out on the lawn that morning. Her father and stepmother stood near the carriage. Each looked as though the cat had gotten their tongues. Clearly, neither felt comfortable.

"Cordelia, you will love the Academy in Nashville, and the city is so exciting. I graduated from there myself, and the coursework is most rigorous," Rachel said, trying to sound the authority on Nashville and the school.

Cordelia offered a forced smile, remembering Aunt Eugenia's instructions to look people in the eye and smile when spoken to.

"Thank you, Mother. I'm sure it is very nice, but couldn't I bring Mammy Cilla with me?" Cordelia asked.

The judge and his wife stared at one another, completely taken aback by Cordelia's request.

"Don't be ridiculous, Cordelia. A darkie has no business in school," laughed Rachel.

The judge answered Cordelia in a kind manner, unlike his wife. "Cordelia, what would Liza Ann, Silas, and Matilda do without Mammy? You mustn't be selfish. They would miss Mammy, and so would we."

Judge Barlow smiled at his wife, but saw no amusement in Rachel Barlow's black eyes. The servants of Absalom Barlow didn't much like the new mistress of Fairview. The goodbyes were sadly given by the slaves at Fairview Plantation. Each one gave Cordelia a small token to remember them. The judge turned to them, admonishing their sullen behavior. "That will be all with the long faces. Cordelia will be back for the holidays. Now, everyone back to work. Cordelia has a long ride to Nashville," Judge Barlow snapped.

He gave his wife a quick embrace, kissing the top of her head.

"I will return shortly. It should only take a couple of days to get Cordelia settled and to finish my business in Nashville, dear."

"Hurry home, Absalom. I don't like being here alone with the darkies. They hate me," Rachel said in a whisper.

Smiling, the judge whispered into her ear, "You have the overseer, Crenshaw, here. You have nothing to worry about."

The judge made his way up into the carriage. "Go ahead, Mordachi. We'd better get a move on," Absalom admonished.

"Yas'r, Judge. Dis here hoss is yo fastest," Mordachi jovially replied.

Turning herself completely around in the carriage, Cordelia waved to Mammy Cilla and Pharaoh. Her stepmother had already walked toward the porch. Silas, Matilda, and Liza Ann ran behind the carriage until it rounded the drive beside the large magnolia at the end of the lane. Cordelia sat close to her father, who, busy looking over his papers, barely noticed her.

Chapter 7

The ride to Nashville was a silent one for Cordelia. Cordelia wanted to ask her father all about her new school, but didn't want to interrupt him. She wanted to show him the angel Pharaoh had made for her. Looking out the small window as the carriage made its way down the bumpy road, she saw a group of slaves repairing a fence along the Nashville Pike. Cordelia couldn't help but wonder what Matilda, Liza Ann, and Silas were doing. Mammy Cilla would probably be working in the kitchen with Nancy and Spicey. How she missed them already!

Cordelia had never seen Nashville before. It was bigger and busier than she had imagined. Peering out the window of the carriage, she saw people coming in and out of storefronts, carrying their purchases. She spied a woman with her children in tow, laughing as they made their way across the street. Soon, they made their way to a large, scary-looking brick building. A tall fence surrounded the property, making it more imposing to the small child. Cordelia suddenly felt afraid, wishing her father had let Mammy Cilla come to school with her.

"Well, here we are, Cordelia," her father announced. "Mordachi, take Cordelia's trunk to the front and wait for us there." Mordachi stepped off the front of the carriage, tipping his cap, saying, "Yass'r, Judge. Let me help you down outta there befo' I gets the trunks." The judge stepped out of the carriage, straightening his frock coat and pants, and Mordachi took the first trunk up to the front door, setting it down carefully, then coming back for the second one. Her father helped Cordelia out of the carriage, then the two walked up to the large double doors, her small hand squeezing the larger hand of her father.

"I'm afraid, Father. Please, don't make me stay here," Cordelia begged, her voice becoming more of a whimper, the tears starting to fall.

"There is nothing to be afraid of, Cordelia. You are going to school, and that is final. Now stop this behavior, you are too old to act this way," Absalom chastised, feeling very uncomfortable with his daughter's emotional outburst.

As they walked through the large doors, an older woman wearing a black taffeta gown approached them, smiling and extending her hand.

"Judge Barlow, I presume. Please, come in," she welcomed. She led them into a large, musty-smelling office. Cordelia surveyed the room, feeling very small among the massive furniture and tall bookshelves lining the walls.

"And this must be young Miss Barlow. Your wife was very excited that there was an opening for your daughter, Judge."

While the adults were talking, Cordelia's gaze was drawn to the large hallway. Two young girls walking past the doorway seemed about her age. Cordelia couldn't remember having a friend who was white in all her young years. She spent most of her 10 years among the adults and slaves at Fairview, save for the trips she made into Gallatin with Aunt Eugenie. She began to think of Liza Ann and Matilda.

Mrs. Lodica Sturgeon made a small coughing sound to get the attention of Cordelia. "Would you like to see your room, Cordelia?" she asked again,clearly annoyed that Cordelia hadn't been paying attention.

"Yes, ma'am. I would like that very much," Cordelia lied.

She felt it was best that she didn't show her disdain of the situation in which she was placed, but rather give in to the hopelessness of it altogether. She walked out of the large office with her father and Mrs. Sturgeon. As they made their way down the hall, she looked at the portraits hanging along the wall. The school had an odd smell, one that reminded Cordelia of her father's law books when she would sit beside him as he worked. She could hear the echo of the nails in the heels of her tight shoes as they walked down the corridor. Before them was a massive stairway. It was wider than the stairway at Fairview, and it had no wall on either side, but was suspended from the second floor above. Cordelia seemed very small, once again.

"When will Cordelia begin her lessons, Mrs. Sturgeon?" Judge Barlow inquired, looking quite pleased with the facilities.

"She will begin first thing Monday morning, Judge. We will get her settled in today and, of course, show her around the Academy. She will be sharing her room with two other young ladies," Mrs. Sturgeon added. Cordelia had never shared her room with another soul. She didn't think she would mind this arrangement, enjoying the closeness Mammy Cilla and Pharaoh's family shared in their cabin at Fairview. Cordelia began to wonder about Mammy Cilla. Would she be thinking of Cordelia, too?

At the end of the hallway, Cordelia saw three older girls walking toward them in single file near the room that was to be Cordelia's. As they passed her, each girl looked down at her, obviously thinking she was a baby. They seemed as old as Mammy!

"Those are the senior ladies. They will be graduating from the Academy in December. As you can see, Judge, the Academy serves young women of all ages."

Judge Barlow smiled, tipping his hat to the girls as they filed past them.

"Mrs. Sturgeon, I have heard only high regards for your Academy. My wife and I are grateful that Cordelia will be getting a fine education here."

Cordelia said goodbye to her father from her new room. Mrs. Sturgeon thought it best that they have privacy to say their goodbyes. She tried to be brave, not wanting her father to be disappointed in her.

"I will be back to Nashville sometime next month. I will check in on you then," Absalom said reassuringly.

Cordelia was used to her father being away for long periods of time, but this was different. She had Mammy Cilla and Aunt Eugenie with her during those times. Now she felt as though she might cry. Cordelia looked down in the large travel bag that she had brought from the carriage. Tucked neatly inside was the doll that her father had given her after he returned from marrying her stepmother. Other mementos that had lovingly been placed were the small doll quilt and angel from Mammy Cilla and Pharaoh. She looked up and smiled at her father.

"I'll see you then," Cordelia replied in a matter-of-fact response.

Cordelia watched from the window in her room as Mordachi helped her father into the carriage. She couldn't remember a time when she was left alone, without the sounds of the family or servants to calm her fears.

As she watched her father's carriage drive away down Church Street, the tears began to drip, first in a plop on the windowsill, followed by a steady flow cascading from her round face onto the floor below. She jumped when two girls came into the room, unaware their new roommate had arrived and was in an emotional state.

"Hello! You must be Cordelia Barlow," the taller of the two girls announced.

Cordelia surveyed the two young girls standing before her. Quickly wiping the tears from her face, she studied them carefully before speaking.

"Yes, I'm Cordelia. Pleased to meet you," she said, somewhat unsure of herself.

The two girls, Suzannah Fraize, of Savannah, Tennessee, and Anna Mosby, of Franklin, Tennessee, were similarly dressed in dark green dresses with their hair in similar braided coiffures.

"Mrs. Sturgeon spoke to us earlier this morning of your arrival, Cordelia. We arrived earlier in the month," Suzannah announced.

Suzannah Fraize was small in stature for her twelve years. Her dark brown hair and pale blue eyes held Cordelia's gaze. She was perhaps one of the prettiest girls Cordelia had ever seen. She shared with Cordelia of her family who were still in Savannah, Tennessee. Her father owned a large plantation and raised cotton and tobacco. She was an only child, like Cordelia. Her parents had paid for a tutor to come from the North to live at their home, but he had recently left to go back to his home in Ohio.

"Pleased to make your acquaintance, Cordelia. My name is Anna Mosby," the taller, blonde-haired girl offered shyly.

Anna Mosby, eleven, was just a few months older than Cordelia. She confided that she lived with her mother and father near Columbia, Tennessee. Her father had a few slaves and a farm. She had two brothers, both of whom attended the military school nearby. She was the youngest child, and this was her first time being away from home.

Cordelia disclosed her life at Fairview to her two new friends. Beaming, she talked about Mammy Cilla, her friends Liza Ann and Matilda, and her mother being in Heaven. As she went on about her life, Anna and Suzannah appeared confused about her admiration for slaves. Before Cordelia could learn more about her new friends, Mrs. Sturgeon appeared in the doorway.

"Cordelia, we will be having evening prayers soon. Anna, would you and Suzannah please help Cordelia put her things away and join us in the chapel?"

Cordelia hadn't even thought about prayers, since the only religion she was accustomed to were the slave services on Sunday morning down behind Old Thomas and Nancy's cabin, beyond the cedar thicket. Her Aunt Eugenia wanted Cordelia to know the stories in the Bible, but that was the extent of her religious training. It would be here, under the guidance of the school's headmaster, that she would get her first religious foundation. Cordelia would learn that the girls of the Academy had little in common with her, but through the friendship with these two, she would forge ahead in this new adventure in her young life.

Each year during Christmas, Cordelia Barlow made the trip home to Fairview. Her friends, Anna Mosby and Suzannah Fraize, had already made the trip back to their own families. It was during the Christmas season of 1858 that Cordelia experienced the death of one of her father's favorite servants at Fairview.

As the carriage made the winding turn from the post road to the long driveway that led to Fairview, a dark foreboding cloud hung over the once happy scenes of Cordelia's home.

Mordachi bounded from the carriage, coming around to help Judge Barlow down first, then offering his hand to Cordelia.

"Judge, what's you think be de matter? Ain't nobody come out to tote yo' trunks," Mordachi said, surveying the yard and beyond.

Absalom surveyed the yard, gazing further to the row of cabins that housed the servants of Fairview. Thin snakes of smoke spiraled from the chimneys, the haze blanketing rooftops.

"Take Miss Cordelia back to the house, Mordachi. I'll walk down to the cabins."

Just then, Rachel Barlow, clutching her wool cape closer to her throat, ran down the steps to her husband. Her tear-stained face caught the attention of Cordelia as Mordachi helped her onto the porch.

"I thought you'd never get here, Absalom! I was so afraid," Rachel sobbed.

Mordachi held the door open as Cordelia walked into the dimly lit foyer. Something wasn't right. Spicey or Nancy always answered the door to take her father's law satchel whenever he returned from a trip. On this day, the house seemed eerily quiet. Cordelia wasn't sure why Mammy Cilla wasn't there to greet her; she always eagerly awaited Cordelia's return home each Christmas. She sat down on the small chair in the foyer, perplexed. Her father and stepmother came into the house, Rachel Barlow still sniffling and wiping her nose on the silk handkerchief she clutched in her hand.

"Rachel, what in Heaven's name is going on?" Absalom sternly inquired.

Rachel, after pulling her husband into the library and closing the large poplar pocket doors, began, her voice shaking, "I'm not exactly sure what happened, but Old Thomas..."

Absalom grabbed his wife by her arms. "What happened to Thomas?"

Rachel continued, "This morning, Mr. Crenshaw found him out by the tobacco barn."

Nothing else needed to be said for Absalom Barlow to understand his wife's meaning. He abruptly turned, opening the doors and walking out of the library. Cordelia watched as her father made his way out of the house. She pulled her woolen cape around her shoulders, feeling the biting chill, and followed him out the door.

Pharaoh met the judge at the door of the cabin, surprised to see the owner of Fairview. "Pharaoh, I've come to see Mammy Nancy and Old Thomas," Absalom said softly.

He entered the cabin, looking at the faces of the servants, some sitting, others standing. In the corner of the room was a pine box resting on two sawhorses that were covered with a blanket. The master of Fairview walked to the coffin to pay his respects.

"Mammy Nancy, what happened?" he asked, touching her shoulder.

Mammy Nancy blew her nose, then spoke,

"He was workin' in de barn, totin' tobacco leaves from de wagon," her voice broke into sobs.

Absalom didn't understand. Thomas knew he didn't have to do manual labor such as this. Peering down into the coffin, he saw a look of peace on the face of his faithful servant.

"I'm so sorry, Mammy Nancy. Thomas was a good man."

Absalom walked over to Pharaoh, pulling him aside. Lowering his voice, he asked,

"Why was Thomas working in the tobacco barn, Pharaoh?"

Pharaoh's eyes met his master's. "Boss Crenshaw, Judge. He tol' Old Thomas he jest a lazy darkie, an' theys no reason he ain't doin' his share.

Absalom Barlow patted Pharaoh on the shoulder and said, "Thank you, Pharaoh."

Standing in the doorway, Cordelia remembered the scene in the cabin from an earlier time, when Pharaoh and Mammy Cilla's little boy, Benny, had been lying in the pine box. Now it was Old Thomas. Mammy Cilla stood and made her way to Cordelia.

"Praise de lawd, it's Miz Cordie. Chile, I sho' have missed you!" Mammy Cilla said, hugging Cordelia tight.

Cordelia took a deep breath as Mammy Cilla pulled her close. The worries of Cordelia's life didn't seem as imposing while she was safe in Mammy's arms.

"I've missed you terribly, Mammy," Cordelia said, giving Cilla a kiss on her cheek.

Pharaoh walked over to the pair. "We sho' has missed you Miz Cordie. Dis is one sad day, but it sho' is good ta' have you home."

Unseen by Cordelia and the others, Judge Barlow walked from the mournful scene, angered by what Pharaoh shared with him. He couldn't abide his overseer or anyone else defying one of his rules. Old Thomas had been with his family for many years, and his faithfulness had earned him a special place at Fairview Plantation. As he made his way down the path to the overseer's cabin, the fury rose within him. *What was Crenshaw thinking, making Old Thomas work in the field like one of the young bucks? He knew Old Thomas didn't have to do fieldhand work.*

Lucas Crenshaw sat staring into the fire, the empty jug of whiskey lying beside him. *Stupid darkie, all them darkies, thinkin' they's special 'cause Judge Barlow's brat acts like one of 'em.*

"Crenshaw, just what in the hell do you think gives you the right to defy me?"

Lucas hadn't heard the judge walk in, and he was startled out of his drunken stupor when the cabin door crashed against the whitewashed plaster wall. He started to rise, wobbling on one leg, but the judge pushed him back to the chair with one shove.

"Now Judge, you yourself gave me the right to do what I think is right where the darkies are concerned. You put me in charge!" Lucas blurted out, suddenly feeling concerned for his safety.

Absalom Barlow's fury over the death of his faithful servant surprised Lucas.

"That *darkie* was one of the servants I brought here with me from my father's plantation. He was too old to be doing fieldhand work and you know it! How dare you defy me!"

The rage that emitted from Absalom Barlow's words frightened Lucas Crenshaw. Barlow's large hands grabbed Lucas' collar, tightening around his throat so that the air was all but cut off from his lungs. Pulling him up from the chair, the judge whispered,

"Don't make the mistake of thinking you are master of Fairview. I'll kill you if you ever make that assumption again, Crenshaw."

When he released him, the chair and Crenshaw made a crash on the bare wood floor. Absalom Barlow had made his point.

The mound of red clay covered the grave of Old Thomas. The mourners began to make their way out of the small slave cemetery at Fairview. Cordelia pulled the wool cape closer to her chin as she stopped for a moment at the wooden marker of her childhood friend, Benny.

"Are you coming, Miz Cordie?" Matilda called from the small procession that left the cemetery.

Cordelia walked through the small wooden gate, closing it behind her.

"Tillie, would you walk with me to Mother's grave?" Cordelia asked.

Matilda drew her thin shawl around her shoulders and walked obediently beside Cordelia. The gravesite of her mother lay just beyond the rose trellis, a place where Cordelia and Matilda had played during her younger days at her father's plantation. The brown grave grass grew above the carving on the headstone, something that bothered Cordelia. Old Thomas always tended to her mother's grave, and now he too lay sleeping beneath the ground.

"Miz Cordie, I'll tend to yur mamma's grave. Don' you worry none about that," Matilda promised, seeing the sadness in her young mistress' eyes.

Cordelia smiled, then looked more serious.

"Thank you, Tillie. I never thought about it before, but why isn't my brother's name on the headstone too?"

Matilda felt the sharp wind against her bare legs. Wishing to be back in her own cabin, she turned to Cordelia.

"Miz Cordie, it's cold, we'd best git back. Mammy and Daddy be wantin' to see you," Matilda coaxed.

Absalom Barlow put his coat and hat on the settee in the foyer and made his way into the parlor. Spicey walked into the room, bringing him a glass of brandy.

"Thank you, Spicey," he said, taking his account journal from the desk. "Would you tell Mrs. Barlow I'd like to speak with her?"

Spicey left the room, walking up to the bedroom where Rachel Barlow had locked herself.

"Miz Rachel, the judge asked fo' you. He be waitin' in the parlor."

Rachel unlocked the door nervously, eyeing Spicey, never turning her back to the servant. She seemed to distrust the servants even more since Old Thomas' death. She pulled the double parlor doors together, walking over to where her husband sat writing in his account ledger.

"I want to discuss the matter of Old Thomas' death with you. Did you hear or see anything out of the ordinary among the servants before his death?"

Rachel Barlow didn't make a habit of listening to the slaves talk, but she was aware of Lucas Crenshaw keeping company with one of the darkies, even the rumors of him being the father of the baby she was carrying. She decided it was best to share the information with her husband.

"Mr. Crenshaw and Molly? Are you certain?" Absalom questioned, disgusted with the thought.

Rachel added, "I overheard Mammy Nancy and Spicey talking before Old Thomas' death. Spicey said Sally must've been waggin' her tongue about young boss Hallert. Does that mean anything to you, Absalom?"

Absalom suddenly felt a sickening in the pit of his stomach, one that he hadn't felt in years. His skin took on a pallor that became apparent to his wife.

"Are you ill, Absalom, are you all right?" Rachel asked, aware of the effect her revelation had on him.

"She said the name *Hallert*? Are you certain?"

Absalom thought that was a name he would never hear again. He had made sure of it, or so he thought.

"Yes, I'm sure that is the name they said. When they saw me, they quickly changed the topic of conversation. But I heard it! What does it mean, and why did you suddenly turn so pale?" Rachel inquired.

Absalom closed his journal, putting the ledger back in the desk drawer. He wiped the perspiration from the top of his lip with the silk handkerchief he had in his breast pocket. In a low, almost inaudible voice he spoke the words, "He was the former overseer here. I had to let him go. He was having an affair with my wife."

Cordelia and Matilda made their way back to the row of slave cabins. Mammy Cilla was leaning over the fire, stirring the coals, when the young mistress and her servant opened the door. Cordelia spied the big quilted bed in the corner, wishing to curl under the warm coverlet and sleep the night away. Mammy Cilla turned, smiling at Cordelia and her oldest child, Matilda.

"I's about ready to send yo' daddy fo' you, girl. You has chores to do. Miz Cordie, yo' papa be lookin' fo' you too," she continued . "Honey chile, you has grown like a weed. You don' gone and growd' up on Mammy! You lookin' mo like yo' mama every day."

Cordelia liked the comparison to her mother. Having no memory of her, she treasured the smallest of details she could get from Aunt Eugenia, which were scant, to say the least. She knew Mammy Cilla had been on the plantation for as long as her own mother. It was only natural, Cordelia decided, that she should ask Mammy Cilla about the baby brother who remained nameless.

"Mammy Cilla, why isn't my brother's name on the headstone with Mother?"

Mammy Cilla had a look of terror overtake her sweet expression. This wasn't lost on Cordelia, and she continued, "Why didn't they put his name on there with Mother?" she repeated.

Mammy Cilla wiped her hands and told Matilda to go up in the loft with Liza Ann.

Obeying without question, Matilda climbed the wooden ladder to the small room overhead. Cordelia sat on the big bed, next to Mammy Cilla.

"Miz Cordie, they's things in this world a young miss don't need ta' worry 'bout. Yo' mama didn't get to give him a name, chile. She went ta' Jesus befo' knowin' she had a baby boy. Now jus' don't be frettin' anymore about it, you hear Mammy?"

Cordelia wasn't satisfied with her explanation, but she knew Mammy loved her and wouldn't tell her lies.

"All right, Mammy, I just wish he had a name. It seems so sad that he wasn't given a name. When I say my prayers at chapel, I don't know what to say when I pray for him and Mama."

Mammy Cilla hated to see Cordelia unhappy, but keeping the past in the past was best for all concerned. It wasn't safe for her to be talking about such things, especially now. Cordelia wasn't a small child any longer, she was almost a woman.

"Miz Cordie, yor' mama loved you very much, that is all you need ta' know. You best go on to de' big house. I'll have Pharaoh walk you up now."

For the remainder of the short visit, Cordelia was bothered by Mammy Cilla's answer. She always felt uncomfortable when Anna or Suzannah talked about their mothers, while she had no memory of hers. She came to the conclusion that her father had buried her mother's memory along with her brother. Why was her family so secretive about everything?

A heavy snow caused the delay of Cordelia's return to classes in January, but the first of February, 1859, she boarded the train from the station in Gallatin. She had grown accustomed to leaving the plantation by herself to return to the Nashville Female Academy and her friends, Anna and Suzannah. This trip would mark the last time she would see the familiar faces from the plantation, those she loved: Mammy Nancy, Mordachi, Liza Ann, Matilda, Pharaoh, and Mammy Cilla. She would remember the tender embrace from Mammy Cilla, and telling her that she loved her best.

Judge Absalom Barlow awoke suddenly from a nightmare. *If Spicey and Mammy Nancy knew about Benton Hallert and Lucretia, did they know about his leaving Fairview? What did Mammy Cilla and Pharaoh know?* Absalom sat up in bed, unaware he had spoken his thoughts aloud.

"Absalom, what's the matter?" Rachel sleepily asked, rolling over to feel the damp sheet that her husband had lain upon.

"It's nothing, dear. Go back to sleep."

Having apparently convinced his wife, Absalom donned his robe and hastily went to his study. He poured a glass of whiskey, and paced nervously as he planned what should be done next. Benton Hallert was dead and gone, and gossiping slaves had no place at Fairview.

The train ride to Nashville was dreary to say the least. The constant pelting of sleet against the windows of the car in which Cordelia traveled only added to the dismal feeling she had upon leaving Fairview. Her father appeared to have aged since her last Christmas visit, and her childhood playmates were busy with their own chores on the plantation. To her dismay, she only had the icy disposition of her stepmother to keep her company.

The railcar had few young ladies her age traveling to Nashville, only those who appeared to be making trips for business purposes, or older couples who were traveling further south from her destination. The passenger who sat beside her, an older gentleman, kept a constant chatter about the foul weather and the upcoming Presidential election. Both of these topics bored Cordelia intensely, but being polite, she smiled and nodded when appropriate. Finally, the train station came into view. Cordelia felt her captivity was soon to end, and she waited anxiously for the conductor to put the stairs down for the passengers to disembark from the car. The gentleman tipped his hat to Cordelia, letting her leave the car before him.

"It was a pleasure talking to you, Miss," he said kindly.

Cordelia made her way down the steps, careful not to catch the hem of her wool cape. As she bent down to pick up her bag, a young gentleman approached her, cautiously.

"Miss Barlow? May I help you with your baggage?" the young man asked.

Cordelia raised her eyes, meeting a most handsome and well-dressed gentleman.

"Yes, I'm Miss Barlow. And you are...?" she curtly inquired.

The two stood, and the young man thrust out his gloved hand.

"Miss Barlow, my name is Gibson Hughes. Your father, Judge Barlow, sent a telegram asking me to meet you at the station this morning."

Confused, Cordelia shook the young man's hand. Studying his face, she tried to remember him. *Could this be Uncle Fredrick's boy?*

Fredrick Hughes had been a frequent visitor to Fairview when Cordelia was a very young child. He had been one of her father's closest friends from nearby Goodlettsville. Fredrick was one of the lawyers the judge held in high regard from the surrounding counties. When the elder Hughes became a father, it was the judge whom he asked to be the child's godfather. Sometime later, Fredrick Hughes suffered a brain hemorrhage, and Absalom Barlow took on the financial duties for the education of the young man, his godson. Now a young man, he was living in Nashville, attending the University and studying to be a lawyer, like his father.

"Yes, I do remember you, Mr. Hughes. But it has been so many years. How did you recognize me?" Cordelia asked.

Gibson took Cordelia by the arm, leading her away from the train and the cloud of smoke that billowed from the locomotive's engine. A young Negro lifted her trunk on top of his shoulder, following the two.

"Well, I have to admit I already asked two other ladies, and they weren't nearly as pretty as you!" he said, jovially.

As the two walked from the train depot, Gibson ushered Cordelia into the awaiting carriage. The two made small talk from the depot to Church Street.

"Thank you for seeing me to school, Mr. Hughes. It was nice seeing a friendly face, and also having help with my baggage," Cordelia remarked sweetly.

"You're most welcome; anything I can do to aid you and your father."

As the carriage stopped, Gibson stepped down, helping Cordelia. The Negro carried the baggage to the steps of the Academy, then waited for the matronly Mrs. Sturgeon to come to the door, letting him inside with Cordelia's belongings.

Anna Mosby stared out the window, watching the two enter the building from the street. She wanted to meet this handsome man, and quickly made her way down to the foyer of the school. Just as Cordelia and Gibson stepped foot on the parquet flooring, Anna Mosby was walking towards them, her blonde hair neatly coiffed in a satin trimmed hairnet.

"Mr. Hughes, this is my friend, Miss Anna Mosby," Cordelia announced, making the formal introduction.

Anna was tongue-tied at the sight of the gentleman before her. Cordelia poked her with an elbow.

"So nice to meet you, Miss Mosby. I see Nashville has its fair share of lovely young maidens!"

Anna blushed, lowering her eyes from Gibson Hughes' gaze. Cordelia, tired from her long train ride, ended the pleasantries.

"Mr. Hughes, thank you for seeing me back to school. I should start unpacking now. It was so nice seeing you again after so many years!" Cordelia exclaimed.

Gibson, not wanting to outstay his welcome, bid both ladies farewell. Before leaving, he turned, saying, "May I come and call on you ladies again in the future?"

Anna looked at Cordelia, imploringly. Cordelia smiled, nodding.

"Of course. Please call again, Mr. Hughes."

As the two watched Gibson Hughes ride off in his carriage, they giggled.

Anna grasped Cordelia's gloved hand in hers, saying, "Cordie, it's positively dreary without you. After you finish telling me all about your Christmas holiday, you must tell me all about Gibson Hughes!"

Anna and Cordelia were soon immersed in their daily routines, not having time to dwell on the handsome Gibson Hughes. They were to be the last happy times Cordelia would have to dwell on for quite some time.

Cordelia wasn't sure why she was being summoned to Mrs. Sturgeon's office. She wasn't aware of any discipline issues for which she was being summoned, perhaps it was due to her upcoming graduation in less than a week. As she stood waiting for Mrs. Sturgeon to open the door, a feeling of excitement overtook her. In less than a month, she would be graduating from the Nashville Female Academy, and soon she would be 18 years old! The look on Mrs. Sturgeon's face snapped Cordelia back into the present rather suddenly.

"Come in, Cordelia," Mrs. Sturgeon said, motioning for her to sit in one of her large leather chairs.

Cordelia sensed by the expression on her face this had nothing to do with her graduation.

"I don't know how to tell you this, I'm so sorry..." she said, her voice breaking into a muffled cry.

"Mrs. Sturgeon, what is it?" Cordelia asked, her heart suddenly in her throat.

"Dear, your mother, Mrs. Barlow, sent a telegram this morning. Mr. Hughes received word early from her, asking him to send word to you."

Cordelia swallowed, feeling a sickening feeling overtake her.

"It's your father, dear. He, uh, well, he has passed away suddenly."

The news took a moment to sink in. "When did it happen? How?" Cordelia asked, feeling the tears streaming down her face.

Mrs. Sturgeon came beside her, putting her arms around Cordelia and hugging her tightly,

"All the telegram said was that he had suddenly passed away, and for you to come as soon as possible. That was the extent of the telegram. I'm so sorry."

For the next hour, Cordelia remained in the office. When she had regained her composure, Anna walked with her back to their room.

"Cordie, would you like me to go along with you? I don't want to see you travel alone," Anna offered.

Cordelia didn't want to take Anna away from her studies, as graduation would be taking place in a few weeks. She didn't have to worry, as later that evening, Gibson Hughes came to escort Cordelia back to Gallatin to say goodbye to her father one last time.

Chapter 11

Cordelia Barlow and Gibson Hughes boarded the afternoon train for Gallatin, Tennessee. The scenery would have appealed more to her if it had not been for the somber occasion on which she was traveling. All along the track, the dogwood and redbud trees dotted the landscape in pink and white splendor. Cordelia still couldn't believe her father was gone. He appeared to have aged when she was at Fairview during the Christmas break, but he didn't complain or appear in ill health.

Gibson Hughes wasn't one to cry, but hearing that his father's closest friend had died saddened him more than he thought. He wiped his eyes with a silk handkerchief that he kept in his frock coat pocket. He chastised himself afterward for not offering it to Cordelia first.

Upon arriving at the train depot, Gibson secured the services of Mr. Drew, a farmer who had come to town to deliver a load of goods. Gibson found out that he lived west of town, but would be glad to take the two out to Fairview, having known Cordelia's father. As Mr. Drew drove his wagon over the dusty road, Cordelia held on to the sides of the wagon seat, while Gibson made use of an overturned crate.

"I heard Judge Barlow had passed, Miss Barlow. I'm sorry for your loss," he offered apologetically.

Cordelia forced a smile, replying, "Thank you. It was quite unexpected. Thank you for driving us home, Sir."

The rest of the ride to Fairview was quiet. Mr. Drew's two mules made their way to the long drive that led from the Nashville Pike to Fairview Plantation. Cordelia strained to see the house ahead of her. The scene reminded her of the trip back when Old Thomas had passed away. The servants weren't in the fields. Perhaps Crenshaw had given them the day off, to bury her father.

"Is there anything I can do, Miss Barlow, before I leave you?" Mr. Drew asked.

Cordelia waited for Gibson to help her from the wagon, and after looking at the large house, looked back and answered, "No, thank you. I appreciate your kindness. "

And with that, Gibson and Cordelia watched as the wagon made its way back down the curve of the drive and past the large cedar trees that lined the entrance.

The massive oak door that had welcomed Cordelia home each Christmas slowly opened, and a pale Rachel Barlow, dressed in mourning, came to the porch.

"Cordelia, your father was buried yesterday. I didn't know if you were coming."

Cordelia couldn't believe what her stepmother was saying. Both she and Gibson looked at one another, then Cordelia began to sob.

Gibson cleared his throat, feeling a lump suddenly rise, causing his voice to crack.

"Mrs. Barlow, we didn't receive word until yesterday. We left within the hour. Why didn't you send word sooner?"

Rachel Barlow stiffened, then continued, "I was here alone, except for the Negras. There was so much to do..."

Cordelia looked up when Rachel's words sank in.

"So much to do? What did you have to do? Where are the servants?" Cordelia snapped.

Cordelia thought it strange that none of her father's servants were milling about.

"Cordelia, why don't you and Mr. Hughes come inside. There are matters that we must discuss. Please, come into the house," Rachel implored.

Cordelia wanted to run, as far as she could, away from the emptiness she was feeling. The grass was just beginning to grow from the warm sunny days that Middle Tennessee was experiencing that May. She looked inside the house, the mourning drape still present. Pulling her arm out of Gibson's, she turned and bolted down the steps. Cordelia trampled over the crocus and hyacinth that grew in the tiny beds Aunt Eugenia had planted years before. The yellow-laden branches from the aged forsythia bushes slapped at Cordelia's dress, catching in her hair as she darted through the woods to the servant cabins. She didn't hear Gibson calling her name.

"Mammy Cilla! It's Cordelia!" Cordelia yelled, not caring that it wasn't proper to shout.

As she entered the cabin door, her spirits sank. It was void of any life; the once warm cabin with Mammy Cilla, Pharaoh, and their children was now empty.

"They's all gone, Miz Cordie," came a voice that sent a chill through Cordelia.

Cordelia turned to see Lucas Crenshaw, a smirk starting to lift the corner of his mouth. Before she could speak, he continued, "All of 'em, sold, outright, to the highest bidder. Good riddance, they was all lazy..."

Before he could finish, Cordelia landed a slap across his face, the impact taking Lucas Crenshaw by surprise, as well as Cordelia. She began to pummel the overseer with both fists, a rage that neither expected.

"Where is Mammy Cilla? Tell me!" Cordelia sobbed, her mind trying to comprehend.

Lucas pushed the girl back, causing her to lose her footing. She fell against the table that was left in the middle of the floor.

"I sold 'em. The whole lot of 'em went down state. The Judge's precious Fairview got sold too. Some uppity Yankee from the railroad bought it, and didn't want the slaves. Humph!" Lucas snorted.

"Who bought them? Where did you send them?" Cordelia screamed.

Lucas laughed, his dark eyes making him more devilish.

"They's down state. You'll never see them again, I venture! I just wanted to see the look on your face when you heard your precious Negras got sold!"

Cordelia stood, wiping her eyes with her hands. Trying to compose herself, she took a deep breath, but the short spasms of breath continued. She couldn't remember hating anyone, but for the first time in her life, she felt hatred for Lucas Crenshaw. She surveyed the cabin, trying to make sense of the nightmare she was living. *Sold? How could father allow selling all of the servants? They belonged to our family. Pharaoh and Mammy were family.*

Speaking without realizing it was aloud, she continued, "Mammy Cilla, I need you. You can't be gone."

Cordelia tried to think. How could she find her father's servants, and more importantly, how could she even buy them? She was just a young girl, and she had no one. Again, the waves of despair overtook her. Through her tears, she saw the one place that held the memory of Mammy Cilla, and the comfort Cordelia so desperately needed. Apparently Pharaoh and Cilla didn't have time to take their bed. Cordelia threw herself down to the soft quilt that had been like a healing balm to her during so many childish woes. Now, it was all that connected her to the loving arms of Mammy Cilla. She breathed in the smell as she buried her face in the soft, worn quilt. She wasn't sure how long she lay on the quilt, but the sound of the door opening brought her back to the present.

"Miss Cordelia, I'm sorry. Your mother sent me to find you. She was concerned," Gibson said, feeling suddenly inadequate in his sympathetic gestures.

"She is not my mother. She is a witch! She said nothing when Crenshaw sold our servants and Fairview!"

Gibson waited, then said, "Mrs. Barlow needs to speak to you, Cordelia. There are things that need to be taken care of before the new owner arrives. I'm sorry, I loved your father too."

Cordelia wondered if her father had loved Gibson Hughes. She never heard her father tell her that he loved her.

"I have to find Mammy Cilla, Gibson. I had so much I wanted to ask her."

"Perhaps your mother, I mean, Mrs. Barlow, can give you that information. Let me walk you back to the house."

Cordelia wanted a moment to gather the quilt and something of Pharaoh's to remember them. Her childhood companions, Liza and Matilda, all gone. It brought the tears once again to her eyes.

Gibson left her, walking back to the house alone. Cordelia carefully folded the quilt, then walked to the wood box beside the fireplace. Inside, was a collection of *whitlin's,* as Pharaoh called them. Cordelia reached down into the box, moving aside the small animals that Pharaoh was so gifted at creating. She spied a mourning dove, so delicate and lifelike. She would take that, fitting as it was. As she turned to stand, something caught her eye on the edge of the tick mattress. A small folded piece of paper lay half in and half out of the underneath side of the tick mattress.

Cordelia crawled partly under the bed, pulling the paper out from beneath the mattress. Rising, she brushed the dirt from her skirt. *Willow Ashby, Columbia, Tennessee. What on earth were Mammy Cilla and Pharaoh doing with this? Who could they possibly know in Columbia?* Why was it hidden in Mammy Cilla's mattress? Cordelia put the paper inside her dress pocket, took the quilt and dove, and closed the cabin door behind her.

Chapter 12

Rachel Barlow's trunks were packed, waiting for the wagon that would take them to the train station in Gallatin. She would leave as soon as she was finished with the business at hand. Cordelia walked slowly into the house, now dark from the drawn curtains. She saw the long table, still covered with the dark sheet from the funeral the day before. She saw her stepmother in the parlor, talking quietly with Gibson Hughes. Hearing Cordelia, she turned.

"Come in, Cordelia. We must talk."

Cordelia walked over to the large French settee that was a favorite spot for afternoon naps in a happier time and took her seat.

"Your father died four days ago. He suffered a stroke. In his will, it was plainly stated that the servants and Fairview be sold. Yesterday, I completed the sale of both."

The words sounded emotionless and cruel, but she sat silently as her stepmother continued,

"Your father had been ill prior to his death, Cordelia. I believe he had a premonition of his death, and therefore made arrangements with an acquaintance from Louisville in regards to the sale of Fairview."

"Mother, where are the servants? Who bought them?" Cordelia asked.

"Mr. Crenshaw took care of that. I had no part of it. Your father had already sold off several prior to his death. Most of those went to a plantation in Chattanooga. I had other matters of more importance than his Negroes."

Cordelia found her voice and sat silent no longer.

"What is to become of me? Did Father make provision for me in his will?" Cordelia asked, almost afraid of the answer.

Rachel Barlow took an envelope from the table. Inside was a small amount of cash.

"After the sale of the plantation and any furnishings I didn't need, your father made it his wish that you receive your portion of his estate upon your twenty-first birthday. Until then, you are given what is in the envelope."

Cordelia opened the envelope, then closed it carefully. She felt as if the air in the room was being taken out, leaving her short of breath. Her stepmother continued, "Cordelia, you will be 18 in less than a month. I know we haven't been close, but if you would like to join me in Nashville after your studies are completed, you are welcome."

The gesture was genuine, and Cordelia was taken aback by her stepmother's sudden act of kindness. At the moment, she had no idea how she would provide for herself. She was too old to be sent to an orphan's home. At least she did have the Nashville Female Academy to call home for another month, but then she would be graduated. Cordelia thought about the sale of all her father's furnishings in the house. That would provide a small fortune, she estimated. She remembered her mother's portrait that was hanging on the wall in the parlor. She walked over to where it was hanging, and without a word, took it from the long golden cord which secured it to the wall.

"I would like to take this, please," she said, hoping there would be no objection.

Rachel Barlow forced a smile. It was only fitting for Cordelia to have her mother's portrait. Rachel had always felt uncomfortable in the presence of the painting.

That evening, as Cordelia lay in her bed for the last time, she felt a wave of panic course through her body. What would she do? She truly hated the thought of living with her stepmother, someone whom she knew had no love for her. Losing her father and without Mammy Cilla to make things all right, her heart sank to a depth she had never known. Crying herself to sleep that evening, she felt utterly hopeless.

After visiting the grave of her father, mother, and brother, she made a final procession past the graves of Old Thomas and Benny, their epitaphs but a mere name crudely carved into the wood. She promised her stepmother that she would come to her home in Nashville after the completion of her schooling.

Cordelia and Gibson were driven to the train depot by Harley, a servant who had belonged to Rachel Barlow prior to her coming to Fairview. The train ride back to Nashville gave Cordelia and Gibson time to discuss the matters of her father's passing. Rachel had given him most of the law books in Judge Barlow's study. He would be inheriting quite a collection. Cordelia learned her father had made provisions for Gibson Hughes, calling him "a son in every way." This hurt Cordelia, but she didn't share her feelings with Gibson. The majority of the trip back to Nashville, Cordelia couldn't help but wonder about the piece of paper she had found in Mammy Cilla's cabin. She decided that she must find out who Willow Ashby was, and maybe it would take her to Mammy Cilla. Perhaps that is who bought her, Pharaoh, and all the other slaves who lived at Fairview. She must go as soon as possible, and the money she received from her father's estate would at least pay for her to hire a driver to take her to Columbia, Tennessee.

Chapter 13

Cordelia finished her term at the Academy a week after the passing of her father. During this time, Cordelia shared her grief with her closest friend, Anna. The girls had been constant companions since Cordelia's arrival at the Nashville Female Academy seven years prior. The girls should have been making plans for their coming out into the social scene. It was the farthest thing from Cordelia's mind. Anna's mother and father had made arrangements to send her brother from their home in Franklin to bring her home. Cordelia shared with Anna the note she found in Mammy Cilla and Pharaoh's cabin. Anna looked at the words, *Willow Ashby, Columbia, Tennessee.*

"Cordie, do you think your mammy wrote this?" Anna asked, studying the note closely.

"Anna, I don't know. I mean, Tillie told me Mammy couldn't read except for her name, however, she could write her name. Nothing more. None of the other servants could read, other than Spicey, our cook."

Anna's bright eyes sparkled with a thought. She looked at her friend, who had taken the note and folded it neatly, placing it on the bedside table.

"Cordie! Why don't you come back to Oak Hill with Mama, Papa, and me? You are more than welcome to stay with us. I know Mama would agree! Then we could help you find this Willow person in Columbia!"

Cordelia wasn't sure how to answer her friend's offer. She didn't want to have to live with her stepmother, that was for certain. Having no one else on whom she could now rely, perhaps this would be a temporary arrangement. Anna also hoped the handsome Gibson Hughes might make a call to check on Cordelia as well!

Following their graduation ceremonies, Anna Mosby and Cordelia Barlow made a call to their friend, Gibson Hughes. Cordelia wanted to thank him for his coming to her aid during the time of her father's passing. Knowing her father thought so highly of him made her want to know more about Gibson. The threesome spent a wonderful afternoon walking and talking together. Anna invited Gibson to her home in Franklin, when he could get away from his studies. Cordelia shared her finding from the cabin as well. The next stop the two made was to a room at the Nashville Hotel. Cordelia's stepmother had taken a room in the house, awaiting a purchase of a more stately home near the capitol building. Cordelia explained that she would be staying for awhile with her friend, and her stepmother agreed. After saying their goodbyes, Cordelia and Anna left Nashville for Franklin, Tennessee on that Friday in May, 1860.

As they rode out of town, Cordelia couldn't help but feel a wave of sadness overtake her. She had been thinking about Mammy Cilla, Pharaoh and their children. Matilda and Liza Ann weren't children any more than she, but to think of them being sold, and not knowing their whereabouts, gave Cordelia a sickening feeling in the pit of her stomach. Never before had the thought entered her mind, that *her Mammy* would be sold. *How could Father do such a thing knowing how much I loved them? Didn't he love me enough to let me have them?* It wasn't until that moment that Cordelia heard herself. Mammy and Pharaoh weren't things that she could have. She wondered if they were being taken care of, not made to do field work at their age. She quickly said a prayer for their safety.

Anna chattered nonstop about Franklin and the people she wanted Cordelia to meet. Cordelia wasn't listening, and Anna poked her in the side with her elbow.

"Cordie, you haven't heard a word that I have said! Mama is giving us a party together! Isn't that grand?" Anna beamed.

Cordelia smiled, trying to sound as excited as her friend.

"It is very exciting! I would like to try and find Willow Ashby, though. I don't think I could enjoy myself until I put the matter to rest. You understand, don't you, Anna?"

Anna's enthusiasm deflated as she took her friend's gloved hand. Letting out a breath as in complete surrender, she acquiesced.

"Of course, Cordie. I'm sorry for being so inconsiderate. Here you've lost your Papa and your Mammy Cilla. I'm sure Papa will spare a driver to take you to Columbia."

The sparkle in Cordelia's eyes returned, even if only slightly. She loved Anna as a sister, and she knew she should be grateful for the Mosby's kind offer to take her in until she could make other arrangements.

"Anna, I promise we will have our coming out party together, and it will be just like we always planned!" Cordelia said confidently.

Cordelia enjoyed the rest of the journey to Anna's home. The rolling hills and large farms reminded her of Gallatin. As the carriage traveled on, she noticed the homes now were farther apart.

"Oh Anna! Who lives in that house?" Cordelia asked.

"That house belongs to Mr. John McGavock. It's called Carnton. Mr. McGavock and Papa are friends," Anna shared.

Finally the carriage arrived at Oak Hill, the home of Evan and Jennie Mosby. The slaves were working in the fields, a sight Cordelia had never given much thought to before her father's death. A large woman, almost as wide as she was tall, came out of the house. She wore a gray dress of simple cotton and a starched white apron. She wore on her head a brightly colored turban, something Cordelia had seen often at Fairview on their servants. She watched the carriage come to a stop, then sauntered over to the door to help Anna and Cordelia.

"Bess! You remember Miss Cordelia? She'll be staying with us," Anna announced.

The servant smiled, careful to remember her manners.

"I sho' do remember you, Miz Cordelia. Miz Jennie says you can have yo' own room. I done fixed it all nice fo' ya," Bess announced.

"Thank you, Bess," Cordelia said, smiling at the Mosby's house servant.

Cordelia remembered how much Anna's parents doted on her. Maybe that is why she didn't refuse their kind offer. She enjoyed being with a family, even if it wasn't her own.

Cordelia spent the next week trying to adjust to life with the Mosby family. They were very kind, but Cordelia couldn't stop thinking about

Willow Ashby. She waited as long as she could, then approached Mrs. Mosby one morning at breakfast.

"Mrs. Mosby, I want to thank you and Mr. Mosby for your hospitality in allowing me to stay with you. I just wish I could repay you," Cordelia said.

Anna had shared with her mother over the years about her friend, Cordelia. Jennie felt that Judge Barlow was a cold, uncaring man. She also felt Cordelia lacked the love from her father that she wanted so desperately. Anna felt sorry for Cordelia, and she would often write in her letters home how sad Cordelia always was.

"Cordelia, you are most welcome. You may stay on as long as you desire," Jennie gifted, glad that Cordelia would be with them.

Just then, Anna joined the two at the table.

"Good morning, Mama, Cordie. Where's Papa?"

Cordelia had hoped to ask if she could travel to Columbia with Anna. She wasn't sure this would be the right time to ask, but looked at Anna, mouthing the words, *Columbia.*

Anna nodded, then asked, "Mama, Cordie and I want to make a trip to Columbia. Would it be all right?"

Jennie sat her cup of tea on the table, looked at both girls, then with a raised eyebrow, inquired, "What on earth is in Columbia, Anna?"

Cordelia spoke up, wanting to tell Mrs. Mosby the truth. She explained the note and how she felt it could be where Mammy Cilla and perhaps the other servants had been sold. Her beseeching eyes struck a chord in Jennie.

"Cordelia, what if this person is unsavory? What if the person you are trying to find is dangerous? It wouldn't be proper for you and Anna to travel to Columbia without an escort."

Anna and Cordelia looked at one another, feeling as if theirs was a lost cause. Then, Mrs. Mosby surprised them both.

"You may go, but you will take Joel. He would be a suitable escort for two young ladies."

Joel Mosby was two years older than Anna. Tall and slender, his dark brown eyes seemed to see into the very depths of one's soul with his gaze. He was the favorite of his mother, even above the pretty Anna, her only daughter. The youngest of her two sons, Joel was soft-spoken and compassionate. Anna had hoped her oldest brother, Jed, would be the choice. He would be busy watching all the young ladies, too busy to keep a careful eye on the two girls.

"Thank you, Mama!" Anna exclaimed, trying to hide her disappointment.

"Yes, thank you, Mrs. Mosby. I appreciate your allowing us to go."

Cordelia and Anna smiled at one another. Their first real excursion! The packing began almost immediately. Joel was summoned from his room to announce his upcoming trip to Columbia. He was less than pleased.

JUNE, 1860

The carriage ride to Columbia was longer than Cordelia imagined. She had never been this far south, and the large plantations that dotted the countryside made her homesick for Fairview. Joel was a quiet chaperone, hardly uttering more than a few words every hour. Anna, on the other hand, chattered nonstop. Cordelia wished for a happy medium between the two. She nodded at the appropriate moments when necessary, and added comments to the topics Anna babbled. Finally, after several hours in the carriage, Joel announced the upcoming town was Columbia. Cordelia poked her head out of the carriage, trying to get a glimpse of the city. The air was fragrant with magnolia blooms and honeysuckle vines that were abundant during the early summer months. Cordelia could feel the sun's rays shining in her eyes; they seemed to kiss her cheeks with their warmth. Anna had grown quiet over the final few miles of their journey, but spoke up when she could see the activity in town.

"Where should we begin our search for this Willow Ashby, Cordie?"

A sudden feeling of panic overtook Cordelia as she realized this might be a wild goose chase. The trio decided it best to pull the carriage over to the side of the street. Joel helped the two girls from the carriage, then instructed Robert, the Negro who drove the carriage, to stay with the horses. They began their walk down the street, searching for someone who might recognize the name Willow Ashby. An older gentleman in a fine beaver top hat made his way toward the three, and noticing they were perhaps lost, approached them.

"Sir, may I ask you a question?" Joel asked, as the gentleman tipped his hat.

"Good morning, young fella. What can I help you with this fine morning?" he asked, his voice sounding as if his fingers had pinched his nostrils together at the ends.

Cordelia and Anna covered their mouths with their gloved hands, avoiding an obvious snicker.

"My sister and her friend are trying to find someone who lives here in Columbia, but we aren't sure where the person lives," Joel shared.

The gentleman appeared puzzled with their question, but felt they were trustworthy.

"Well, I have lived in Columbia most of my life, so I suppose I could possibly help you. Who is this person the ladies are searching?"

Joel presented his sister and friend to the gentleman, then Cordelia said, "I am trying to find Willow Ashby. Do you know this person?"

A smile began to overtake his face. Nodding, he said, "Oh yes, I know Mrs. Ashby. Fine lady. What business do you have with her?" he asked, clearly watching out for his friend.

Cordelia wasn't sure how to reply, for fear he would think they meant Mrs. Ashby harm or were making up the whole story. Joel spoke up, saying, "Sir, my friend's father recently passed away, and Willow Ashby might be the person who purchased his servants. We don't want to bother her, but we'd like to talk to her. Nothing more."

The gentleman could see the desperation in Cordelia's eyes, and reached out his hand to grasp Cordelia's.

"Young lady, I'm not sure if Willow Ashby is the person you are searching for, but I don't believe you are meaning her any harm. I would be happy to direct you to her home. It isn't far from here," he ventured.

The carriage followed the unnamed stranger to 312 West 7th Street. When the carriage stopped in front of the house, the gentleman departed from his carriage. He helped Cordelia and Anna, then said, "I'm sorry I don't have time to make introductions for you, as I am late for a meeting. It was nice meeting you. My name is Robert Farnsley."

Cordelia took the gentleman's hand. "I am so grateful for your help, Mr. Farnsley."

Joel and Anna Mosby thanked Mr. Farnsley, then waited as he left in his carriage.

"Well, shall we, ladies?" Joel asked, motioning to Anna and Cordelia.

Cordelia surveyed the magnificent house that stood before them. It was nothing less than a showplace. The Victorian Second Empire home was red brick with lovely white Italianate marble curved window crowns and a gray slate mansard roof. Inserted within the slate tiles were beautiful patterns in gold and red. The central tower of the structure was made more dramatic by the circular window at the third story, where a cupola adorned the top. Cordelia couldn't help but notice the large bay window which jutted out from the lower level. The long walk from the street to the house was brick, and two large magnolia trees flanked each side of the stately home. Cordelia felt certain Willow Ashby could afford the servants, but a home in town would have no need for the field workers, only those who would tend the gardens and lawn. As they approached the massive door, which recessed back from the entrance, Cordelia grabbed Anna's hand in hers. Joel stood behind the two girls, waiting to see which would knock on the massive door. Finally, he reached between the two and grabbed the brass knocker, turned to Cordelia and said, "Cordie, Anna and I feel it best that we should let you meet Mrs. Ashby alone. We will be with Robert in the carriage should you need us."

"Yes, perhaps it would be best. She might not trust three strangers showing up unannounced."

Cordelia's heart skipped a beat when the door parted, slightly at first. After what seemed like an eternity to Cordelia, the door opened to a small Negro servant.

"Good mornin'," the servant said politely.

Cordelia spoke up, saying, "Good morning. I was hoping to speak with Mrs. Ashby."

The servant didn't open the door any wider, but asked, "Who should I tell Miz Ashby is callin' today?"

Cordelia smiled her best smile, introducing herself. "Please tell her that Cordelia Barlow would like to speak with her."

The Negro servant stepped aside, motioning for Cordelia to enter the large entryway.

"Yo'r welcome ta' wait in de parlor. Jest' a minute."

With that, she left her to admire the furnishings in the ornate parlor. Cordelia noticed a lovely piano that sat against the far wall. She had never learned to play, as her stepmother never gave her lessons on the one in the parlor at Fairview. On the wall above the mantle hung a beautiful portrait of a young woman. Something about the woman seemed oddly familiar, but Cordelia wasn't quite sure what it was. She noticed the beautiful harp that sat in front of the large bay window. Just as she was about to touch the harp, the Negro servant entered the room.

"Miz Ashby say she can see you now. She 's out in da' garden. You kin' follow me," the servant instructed, and Cordelia obediently followed her down the long hallway.

On each side of the hall were different rooms, all decorated in fine furnishings. Cordelia seemed to be gliding across the floor to keep up with the servant. She led her through a doorway in the back of the house which opened onto a covered porch. Beyond lay the most beautiful garden Cordelia had ever seen. Large trees gave the appearance of a canopy that covered a portion, where smaller, more manicured bushes and trees graced a lawn that was obviously tended carefully by her servants. The smell of roses captured Cordelia's senses. She looked about, taking in the lovely area behind the magnificent house. The carriage house was fashioned as stately as the main house, and a rectangular brick building, which she assumed was the kitchen, sat to the left of the house. Another smaller building was located to the rear of the manicured garden. She glanced at the faces of the servants who were working in the garden, but none were familiar to her.

Abruptly, the young servant stopped in front of a lady who had her back turned to Cordelia. She was busy snipping buds from a gardenia bush that grew next to a rock wall. The servant announced, "Ma'am, I brung Miz Barlow to you."

The petite woman standing before Cordelia appeared to be in her late forties, perhaps. Her eyes were the deepest shade of green, and presently the sunlight gave the appearance of gold flecks dancing from them. Her dark black hair showed no signs of her age, having a youthful shine. Her neatly coiffed tresses were braided from the severe center part, joined together at the nape of her neck in a dark, beaded net. From her ears hung delicate earbobs of garnet, matching the broach at her collar. Cordelia noticed the dark green and burgundy plaid frock was fitted tightly at the waist, around which she wore a dark belt. The chatelaine that was attached from her belt held two keys and a small pocket watch. Cordelia remembered her Aunt Eugenia having a similar one on which the keys of the sugar chest hung. Thinking of a pleasant memory caused her to smile, and then she noticed that she too was being assessed.

Willow Ashby looked as though she were seeing a ghost before her, not noticing Cordelia's appraisal of her appearance. Quickly, she remembered herself.

Turning to her servant, she gestured kindly.

"Thank you, Martha. Why don't you bring our guest a glass of lemonade. I believe a cold refreshment is in need by all today."

She motioned for Cordelia to sit with her under the shade of the gazebo. Wisteria vines covered the roof and sides, giving it a most pleasant atmosphere in which to recline.

"So, you're Cordelia Barlow?" Willow said, studying every inch of Cordelia's face.

Cordelia felt uneasy with the way in which Willow stared at her features.

"Mrs. Ashby, I wanted to speak with you about a note I found."

Willow sat quietly, unsure of what was about to be shared with her. From the reticule Cordelia was carrying, a small folded piece of paper was brought out for Mrs. Ashby to hold. Taking the paper, her hands began to tremble. As she opened the folded paper, words written long ago stared back at her. Cordelia watched nervously as Willow Ashby finally spoke.

"Where did you get this?" she inquired, as the memory of the day it was written came back to her.

"I found it. I was hoping you were the person who purchased my father's servants. Did you purchase the slaves sold at Fairview, my father's plantation?" Cordelia inquired.

Not sure how to begin, Willow Ashby folded the paper and handed it back to Cordelia.

"I'm sorry, Cordelia. I didn't purchase the servants from Fairview. But the paper is in my hand."

Now it was Cordelia who was perplexed. *How did Mammy Cilla get the paper?*

Willow Ashby took Cordelia's hand in hers. She spoke kindly, softly, "I gave Priscilla the paper when I left Fairview. I was with your mother when she passed away."

Cordelia couldn't believe her ears. *Why didn't Mammy Cilla tell her about Willow?* Other questions immediately came to mind as Cordelia let the information sink in. *Who is this Willow Ashby?*

"Who are you?" Cordelia asked, almost afraid to hear her reply.

Willow chose her words carefully, then began to explain.

"My name is Willow Dryer Ashby. Your mother, Lucretia, was my only sister," she said.

Cordelia started to speak, stopping, as Willow continued, "Your father was gone most of the year, traveling as a circuit judge in the surrounding counties in those days. Your mother sent for me when she felt her time of confinement was near. You were just a small, little thing, still a baby yourself."

Cordelia listened without saying a word, wanting to hear more about her mother.

"I had a daughter myself then, just shy of seven when your mother sent word that she needed me. I stayed almost a month, after which time your mother passed from the childbirth fever."

At that point, Cordelia interrupted, "And my brother, the baby who died?"

Willow paused, then continued. Her words were guarded and carefully formed as she referred to Judge Absalom Barlow.

"Cordelia, your mother wanted me to take you with me, back here to Columbia should anything happen to her. It was her wish. When your father returned and found that Lucretia had not survived the birth, he flew into a rage. He and your mother had been estranged, and he resented my coming."

Willow paused, allowing time for the news to sink in fully. Whether it had, she wasn't sure. Finally, Cordelia spoke.

"And Father wouldn't allow you to take me? Is that when Aunt Eugenia was brought to come live with us?" she asked.

Taking in a deep breath, Willow explained further. "Dear, I begged your father to let me raise you, your own mother's sister. But he refused. He also forbade me to contact you any further. He wanted nothing more to do with your mother or her family."

The words stung Cordelia, bringing tears to her eyes. She always felt her father had tried to forget her mother, save for the portrait that hung in the corner of the parlor. Finding her voice, she brought herself to ask the question Willow had hoped she would not.

"Why did Father hate my mother so?" she squeaked, the emotion rising in her throat.

Willow leaned in to take both of Cordelia's hands in hers. Looking into the tear-filled eyes, she continued, "Your mother had been unfaithful with the overseer there. He was punishing her and you for this indiscretion."

Cordelia could hardly fathom her mother in this light. She had always imagined her mother in Heaven, angelic, not adulterous. She couldn't, wouldn't believe it!

"That's a lie! Mother would never! You're lying!" Cordelia snapped.

Willow moved closer, seeing the servants rising from their labors after hearing the outburst. She said, "I loved my sister, Cordelia. I would not repeat this if you hadn't come looking for me. But you must know the truth! Your father did away with that overseer, and that is why I didn't challenge him. I feared for your safety."

Cordelia quieted, taking in all that her aunt was telling. She had heard about an overseer, only briefly, when the servants thought she was out of earshot. She remembered how Mammy Cilla and Mammy Nancy would comment about the goings on while the judge was away. *Could this be what they meant? Did Father commit murder?*

"You must tell me, did father kill the overseer? I must know."

Willow let out a sigh. With all she had within her, she continued, "Priscilla and Nancy saw Absalom returning from the overseer's cabin the night before I left. He had some sort of tool in his hand, and they said it was covered in blood. The next morning, the servants were told there would be a new overseer. Benton Hallert had left suddenly to take care of a family emergency. That was when Priscilla came to me. Fearing something might happen, I gave her my name and address on a slip of paper. I told her when you were old enough, make sure you got the paper to come find me."

Cordelia remained silent. The shock of this news was more than she expected. How could her father have committed murder? She never expected to learn such revelations regarding her mother and father. Her mother, the one person she dreamed was in Heaven; now, she wasn't even sure of that. What kind of man was Absalom Barlow? *Is that why he had never shown her real love?* All she could do was bury her head in her hands and sob.

After a time, Willow patted Cordelia on her shoulder. Knowing this was too much for even an older woman to fathom, she wanted to give Cordelia all the time she needed to compose herself before deciding whether she wanted to continue this visit or leave forever. Willow stood, smoothing down her taffeta skirt. Cordelia raised her head, her eyes and nose both a mess.

"Here, take my hankie and dry your eyes. You should never be without one, dear," Willow said kindly. "I know you have more questions. Let's go inside and get out of this morning sun. We'll be as brown as Martha if we don't get indoors!"

Cordelia obediently followed her aunt into the large house. Coming in from the bright sun left her partially blind in the semidarkness of the house. Cordelia followed her aunt down the central hall that led to the front of the house. She was led into a smaller parlor, opposite of where she waited earlier that morning. Willow turned and closed the pocket doors behind them.

"Would you like to ask your friends to come in for the evening? There is so much we have to talk about. You must stay here, with me. I'm sure they are wondering what has become of you," she offered.

Cordelia wasn't sure what to say to this offer. Part of her wanted to run out the door, never to return to Willow Ashby. However, it was her strong, determined part that wanted to stay and talk more with Willow Ashby, so she agreed.

"Thank you, Mrs. Ashby, for your kind offer. I would very much like to talk more about my mother and Mammy Cilla," Cordelia replied quietly.

Willow could sense a veil of caution that kept a wall between Cordelia and herself. She wanted to take this child in her arms and love her for all the years she felt no one cared. But for now, she would let Cordelia feel welcomed.

Cordelia and Anna spent the evening in one of the five bedrooms in Willow Ashby's home, with Joel in the room next door. Cordelia did not share all she had learned with Anna, only that Willow was her mother's older sister. After a long discussion, Cordelia decided she would remain for a few days with Willow, then decide her future. The next morning, Joel and Anna ate their breakfast with Cordelia, then thanked Mrs. Ashby for her hospitality. Cordelia walked them to the carriage where Robert was waiting to drive them home to Oak Hill.

"You know you are welcome to stay with us, Cordie. Mama and Papa have already said you are one of the family," Anna chimed merrily.

Joel finished helping Robert with their baggage, then joined in.

"If you need me to come for you, send a letter to the post as soon as possible. Good luck, Cordie."

After the two girls hugged several more times, Cordelia Barlow waved goodbye to her dearest friend in the world. Looking back at the large house, she set her mind on having a long discussion with Willow Ashby.

That afternoon, Willow and Cordelia spent several hours in the small parlor with the sunny bay window. The breeze blew the long billowy curtains, giving them a ghostly appearance. Cordelia had listened attentively as Willow Ashby told her of the Dryer family history, her grandparents' names, and brought out her family Bible. Inside, the names of several generations were neatly written, along with annotations of family history. Cordelia noticed several photographs in small cases that were of children displayed on a small table, along with two larger portraits that hung on the wall. Willow saw her curiosity, and said, "That is your cousin, Emma. She died when she was 12 years of age. She would have been 23, had she lived."

As Willow remembered this young child who was taken during a cholera outbreak, a brief moment of melancholy overtook her. Such a beautiful life, cut down in the flower of youth. Her grief would be compounded by the loss of her husband to the disease as well the following week.

"What happened to her, Mrs. Ashby?" Cordelia asked.

Willow explained her untimely death, then suggested, "Cordelia, you may call me Aunt Willow. I would like that."

Cordelia smiled. Her mind quickly conjured up another aunt. She had to laugh to herself at the thought of these two aunts and how very different they appeared.

"Emma was very pretty. I wish I could have known her."

Cordelia saw another photograph which caught her eye. It was a small boy, standing on a chair. Before she could ask, her aunt volunteered, "That is my son, Simon. He is a little younger than you are, Cordelia."

"Is he...alive?" Cordelia reluctantly asked.

Willow's face took on a brightness when she spoke of him. Her smile was something Cordelia found infectious, causing her, for the first time, to genuinely smile back.

"Oh yes, very much so! He attends the Western Military Academy, in Nashville. His father would have been so proud," Willow exclaimed, a tone of sadness in her voice.

Cordelia looked more closely at the faces in the golden frames. She couldn't remember ever seeing a portrait of herself displayed. She remembered the special trips with Aunt Eugenia to Gallatin for the reason of having a portrait taken by the funny box. She wondered where those portraits were now. Then she remembered the portrait of her mother.

"I have a portrait of Mother. It is all that I have of her," Cordelia said.

Willow remembered the portrait, and was thankful Cordelia was able to take it when she left Fairview. Cordelia listened to the stories Willow shared about her mother growing up at the plantation of Dryer Hall.

Cordelia wanted to hear more about her mother, and Willow tried to remember as many recollections that she could, careful to avoid anything that would lead them to her involvement with the overseer, Benton Hallert.

The rest of the week proved to be enjoyable to Cordelia. As much as her heart was saddened by her recent losses, she began to let the wall she had placed around herself crumble gradually. In Willow, there was security, something she felt with Mammy Cilla. By the end of the week, she sent a letter to Anna Mosby asking for her trunks to be sent to Columbia, along with a letter thanking the Mosby family for the care and hospitality displayed during her time of need. She explained her place was with her mother's sister until she could live on her own. Anna was crestfallen at the news, but understood Cordelia's need to find happiness after the sale of Fairview and the passing of her father. Finding Mammy Cilla, Pharaoh, and the others plagued Cordelia's thoughts.

Willow didn't share with Cordelia the real reason for her absence in her life. Lifting the lid to a small velvet-lined box she kept inside her glove drawer, she removed a yellowed piece of paper. The letter was sent from Judge Absalom Barlow, and within the envelope was the letter Willow Ashby had sent pleading for the judge to allow Cordelia to come to Columbia. He told her no further correspondence would be necessary; Cordelia had passed away from scarlet fever that winter. Willow thought it best not to share this with Cordelia. How could she tell Cordelia how cruel her father was? Perhaps she already knew.

Living in her aunt's home soon gave Cordelia a peace about her future. She wondered about the cousin who was attending a military school in Nashville. Perhaps she would accompany her aunt when she went later in the summer to visit him. Cordelia enjoyed exploring the large house; her favorite room was the ballroom on the third floor. Willow sent invitations for a grand party introducing Cordelia to Columbia society. She invited several of the young ladies from the Athenaeum Girls School, most of whom were a few years younger than Cordelia. It was the first time Cordelia felt special, other than when she was around Mammy Cilla. Anna Mosby made a special trip to Columbia to stay the week with her friend. The two girls practiced their dance steps with two dressmaker's forms. Cordelia had never seen such a beautiful home, and she was proud to show all of it to her best friend, Anna. Willow called in her dressmaker, Louisa, a petite Negro who had asked to be purchased by Willow's husband when her owner beat her regularly. She had been with Willow for almost 30 years. She was a gifted seamstress, and many of the ladies in Columbia came to Louisa to stitch a gown. The new gown she fashioned for Cordelia was the most beautiful article of clothing she had ever seen. She truly was the belle of the ball, all of her dances taken by the young gentlemen from Columbia. Disappointed that Gibson Hughes wasn't on the guest list, Anna tried to enjoy the gaiety of the evening.

As the spring days turned to summer, Cordelia became a constant companion to Willow. Under her aunt's tutelage, Cordelia learned the art of being a charming hostess and graceful dancer. She accompanied Willow to services each Sunday morning across the street at St. Peter's Episcopal Church, where she prayed that the Lord would watch over Pharaoh and Mammy Cilla. Cordelia found Willow to be God's answer to her prayer that she be loved. She would never forget Mammy Cilla, however, and the love she felt for her.

After Cordelia had been with Willow for two months, the pair set off for Nashville. It would be Cordelia's first excursion with her aunt, but more importantly, the first time she would meet Willow's son, Simon. She would make a stop by the Female Academy, wanting to introduce her aunt to Mrs. Sturgeon. She also wanted to make a call on Gibson Hughes. The carefree days that she enjoyed staying at the home of Willow Ashby would be something to look back upon in more perilous days that were to come.

NASHVILLE, TENNESSEE, AUGUST, 1860

Nashville was what some called the Athens of the South. Cordelia had grown up in the city, attending the Female Academy. She took for granted the grand homes and buildings that dotted the city. The railroad had been central to the city prospering, connecting the city to points north in Louisville, Kentucky, and to points south, near Atlanta, Chattanooga, and Memphis. The slave trade continued to flourish, with Nashville being one of the largest procurers of slaves in the South. Cordelia wondered as they passed the law offices what might have become of the servants at Fairview after her father's death. A tall man with a frock coat and top hat made his way out of the building, two dark-skinned men following closely behind. She wondered who owned Pharaoh, Mammy Cilla, and their children now.

Willow led Cordelia and Martha from the train depot to an awaiting carriage. She paid the driver to take them to the Military Academy. As the carriage made its way down the street, Cordelia's thoughts traveled to Gibson Hughes. The last time they were together was just a few months before, and she had just learned of her father's death. It seemed he knew Absalom Barlow better than his own daughter. *Did he know the real Absalom Barlow?*

The carriage stopped at the front gate of the Western Military Academy. Willow leaned forward, speaking to the driver. "We are going to be paying a visit to my son. Could you be back to drive us to another destination in, say, two hours?"

The driver tipped his hat and agreed. He hopped down from his perch on the front of the carriage, offering his hand to first Willow, then Cordelia. When Martha stood to disembark from the carriage, he turned and situated himself in the seat once again. Martha said something under her breath, which Cordelia pretended not to hear.

Willow took Cordelia's arm in hers, a gesture becoming familiar to her. She smiled at her aunt, whose expression always seemed to be like the carved angels in the cemetery in town. As they walked closer to the entrance, Willow shared how excited she was for Cordelia to finally meet her cousin, Simon.

Simon Ashby had eagerly awaited the arrival of his mother. Just shy of 17 years old, he appeared much older. His once-long curls were now trimmed to a short military-style cut. His face had lost the boyish chubby cheeks, and now showed signs of chin whiskers that were recently shaved. His deep green eyes must be a family trait, as Cordelia and her aunt both had a variation of green. He appeared to be taller than his mother remembered, standing at least a foot above his mother's five foot, two inch frame. He saw his mother and his nurse, Martha, then noticed a pretty girl accompanying them.

"Mother! Aunt Martha!" Simon exclaimed, rushing down the paved walkway.

Willow and Martha walked ahead of Cordelia, showering the young man with hugs and kisses, which he tried to keep to a minimum, in case other cadets were watching. Following the reunion, Willow motioned for Cordelia to join them. She smiled her best smile, looking her cousin squarely in the eye, as she had been taught. Willow introduced her young niece.

"Simon, this is your cousin, Cordelia Barlow. She will be staying with us."

Simon tipped his cap, bowing at Cordelia. The dimple in his chin caught her eye when he once again stood upright.

"Pleased to meet you, Cordelia. I hope you will enjoy your stay with Mother," Simon jovially offered.

Following their formal introductions, the group made their way into the barracks to finish their visit. Simon would be starting his last year at the Western Military Academy. It was apparent the other cadets were talking about the upcoming election. The ladies didn't want to hear about politics, but the mood of the Southern states left little doubt what was to happen should Lincoln get elected in the fall. Willow had read the paper and the sentiments of the South. The state was divided in both its allegiance and the views on secession.

Their visit was too short for Willow's liking, but Simon was expected to report to his classes. After a loving embrace from both his mother and Martha, Simon gave Cordelia an awkward hug.

"Cousin Cordelia, it was so nice to meet you. I look forward to seeing you when I come home for the Christmas holiday," Simon offered, his voice now much deeper than his mother remembered.

Cordelia thanked Simon, finding him to be as thoughtful and sincere as his mother. As the three women made their way down the sidewalk and through the entrance to the Military Academy, Cordelia saw a familiar face carrying a box of books toward the building they had just left.

"Mr. Hughes! We were just on our way to see you!" Cordelia beamed.

Gibson Hughes was just as surprised to see Cordelia. His excitement wasn't lost on Willow. He tipped his hat, and Cordelia bowed slightly. Etiquette courses were a yearly ritual at the Female Academy, and Cordelia had been given a refresher course under Aunt Willow's tutelage. Cordelia introduced Gibson to her aunt.

"Mr. Hughes, this is my aunt, Mrs. Ashby."

Gibson acknowledged Willow politely, then added, "Mrs. Ashby, I believe I have met your son, Simon. I attend the University, and recently inquired about transferring into the Military Academy."

This was a surprise to Cordelia. Willow spoke softly, always genteel in her mannerisms.

"It is a pleasure meeting you, Mr. Hughes. My niece has spoken highly of you. We hope you will come to Columbia and visit sometime soon!"

Cordelia was thankful her aunt extended an invitation to Gibson. She would like to have an opportunity to get to know this young man better. As the three talked briefly, Cordelia learned that Gibson was taking the box of books to one of his instructors. He was late, and would have to excuse himself from the unanticipated, but delightful meeting. He bid farewell to all three women. Martha watched the young man walk away, then said to her mistress, “He sho’ is handsome. Miz Cordie, he sho’ is a fine young man.”

Cordelia blushed, and a warm tide seemed to cover her throat and face at Martha’s words. Willow admonished Martha, “Now Martha, I’m sure Miss Cordelia hasn’t been lost on the pleasant features of Mr. Hughes.”

Just then, their carriage pulled alongside the walkway, and the driver disembarked to help the ladies. The ride to the Nashville Hotel took but a few moments, and Willow and Cordelia enjoyed seeing so many people coming and going within the city. Cordelia had grown to love the city, but found she desired the pastoral setting in which Columbia was situated far more.

Martha sat silently, watching a scene unfold from just beyond their destination. Martha had seen the storefront on other trips to the train depot, but today something pulled her attention to watch with intense interest. Willow and Cordelia were talking about Simon, and neither noticed the small wagon of slaves being taken from the warehouse to the train depot. The faces of the slaves showed little emotion. Cordelia had not seen the faces she knew from childhood riding slowly away from her.

Chapter 17

The Presidential election of 1860 found the candidates Abraham Lincoln and Hannibal Hamlin the winners. Having received not a single vote in the state of Tennessee, it was apparent the state did not support the platform of the new Republican Party. Talk of secession had been on the lips of many a Congressman from the South for over a year, and now, the state of South Carolina had made good on its threat.

Preparations for Simon Ashby's homecoming during the Christmas holiday of 1860 would be a happy time for Cordelia. The loss she had incurred over the past year only briefly dampened her happiness. She had been given a sunny room on the east side of Willow Ashby's home. The morning sun felt warm on her face as she sat at her dressing table that morning in December. Setting near her brush and mirror were the angel and mourning dove that Pharaoh had carved. Lovingly, she touched each, thinking of Pharaoh's kind smile and deep voice. The memory of his singing while he worked brought a smile to Cordelia. The tune came out in a soft hum, and then she began to sing.

As she rounded the top landing of the second floor stairway, Willow recognized a familiar melody that she had once heard, many years ago. She remembered her own mammy sang the same song.

"I had forgotten that song, Cordelia. I haven't heard it since I was a young girl at Dryer Hall," Willow remarked.

Cordelia smiled. She remembered the story of Pharaoh's mother, Dolly. She had been the mammy to Lucretia and Willow Dryer.

"I miss our servants singing, especially when Old Thomas would play his fiddle," Cordelia reminisced.

Willow noticed the angel and dove sitting on the dressing table. She leaned down to get a closer look.

"These are lovely, Cordelia. Who made them for you?" she asked.

Cordelia handed the dove to her aunt. As Willow turned the delicate bird in her hand, Cordelia answered, "Pharaoh made the angel for me many years ago. I found the dove in his box of whitlin's when I went back after Father died."

"His work is lovely. I'm sorry that you weren't allowed to see him and Mammy Cilla before they were sold," Willow said.

Cordelia took the dove and sat it back on her table. Rising from her chair, she gave her aunt a hug.

"Thank you, Aunt Willow. I miss them terribly."

Willow had almost forgotten the purpose for her trip upstairs. She took Cordelia's hands in hers,

"Cordelia, Simon will be home at the end of the week. I would like to have a Christmas Ball to welcome him, and I'd like you to help me with the hostess duties."

Cordelia was excited to have another social event at her aunt's home so soon.

"Of course, Aunt Willow. I'll be happy to help you," Cordelia happily offered.

The two made their way downstairs to begin the preparations for Simon Ashby's homecoming. The house servants began decorating the house with evergreen boughs and bows. Willow had Lewis bring down Elijah Ashby's sword to be polished. Elijah had carried that sword with him to Veracruz during the Mexican War, as a young soldier fighting with General Winfield Scott. It was handled as reverently as the minister held the communion chalice. It would one day be given to Simon. Willow sent Martha to the telegraph office that afternoon. She wanted two invitations for Simon's Christmas Ball to reach the recipients as quickly as possible.

On the morning of December 20th, Willow sent Lewis to the train depot to meet Simon. The house was festively decorated with two Christmas trees that year. Cordelia remembered Christmases at Fairview, and this was the first Christmas she had spent away from her childhood home. Sitting in the front parlor, she looked out the large bay window at the street below. She recognized the carriage driven by Lewis, and saw the familiar face sitting beside her cousin. *What is he doing here?* Startled by the voice behind her, Cordelia jumped.

"Dear, I took the liberty of sending a telegram to Mr. Hughes. I thought he would enjoy a visit to Columbia for the holidays," Willow said, a mischievous smile overtaking her small, delicate face.

Cordelia's attempt to seem less than enthused amused her aunt. She stood from her seat, saying, "That was very considerate of you to think of Mr. Hughes, Aunt Willow. I'm sure he will find Columbia as welcoming as I have."

Willow remembered the look in their eyes that afternoon at the Military Academy. Cordelia Barlow wasn't fooling anyone.

The servants lined the hallway to welcome young Simon home for the holiday break. Gibson Hughes looked beyond the servants for Cordelia. He had been looking forward to seeing the daughter of the late Judge Barlow again.

Cordelia had excused herself from the front parlor. She heard the voices of Jethro and Martha receiving their young master as he entered the festively decorated house. Willow had closed the parlor doors, following Cordelia into the exuberant exchange.

"Welcome home, Masta' Simon. We sho' has missed ya!" Jethro exclaimed.

"Thank you, Jethro. It's good to be home, I've missed you all."

Willow had ownership of six slaves. Martha, in her late forties, had been her personal maid since she was a young woman. Louise had been purchased after Willow witnessed her drunken owner beating her for refusing his advances. Lewis was her husband's manservant, coming with him to Columbia from his parent's home near Murfreesboro. Jethro, the gardener, was the husband of Esther, the cook and laundress. Cyrus, the youngest of the servants, had been with Willow for only a short time. He had run away from a steamboat that had sunk near Memphis. A family had brought him as far as Columbia, when he tried to run away again. Willow had need for a groom for her two gray mares, and thought Cyrus could learn a trade from Jethro. He was only seven years of age then, and now, the strapping young man was a year older than Simon.

The table in the large dining room had been set for four. Martha, Lewis and Esther brought the bowls into the room and sat them on the large sideboard. A large ham had been baked, and the smell wafted throughout the room. The silverware gleamed under the glow of the brightly lit chandelier. Willow's family Wedgwood china adorned the table. It was usually kept in the ornately carved hutch that had been Willow's mother's. A crackling fire gave the room a warm glow, with the pastel blue walls giving off a yellow glow.

"Mr. Hughes, we are most anxious to hear about your family back in... where did you tell Cordelia you are from?" Willow inquired, glancing at Cordelia when she spoke.

Cordelia smiled, waiting for Gibson Hughes to respond. As the food was being served onto the plates, Gibson shared that his family had been living in the Goodlettsville area for several generations. Esther waited for Willow to nod that it was time to offer the blessing. The servants stood, heads bowed, as Willow said a prayer of thankfulness for the return of Simon, the arrival of Cordelia to her home, and the new acquaintance in Gibson Hughes. Following the prayer, Simon began to discuss the talk among the cadets and their instructors regarding the election of Abraham Lincoln. Willow had not escaped the talk of the ladies at the church and the editor of the *Maury Press*, who often gave his opinion of the direction the Southern states were moving.

"Mother, there is going to be a vote soon for secession. Everyone is talking about it," Simon announced excitedly.

Willow didn't want to talk of secession. But the two young cadets at her table had an air of enthusiasm that lent itself to youth.

"Simon, we should pray that the country doesn't tear apart over the election," Willow admonished.

Cordelia had been listening to the conversation, wondering why anyone would be interested in politics. She quietly ate her yams and sliced ham. Gibson tried to appear engaged in the talk of secession, however his gaze continued to turn in the direction of Cordelia.

"Mrs. Ashby, one of our instructors, Col. Bushrod Johnson, even thinks we will soon be taking a vote to secede from the Union. The vote could happen as soon as the first of the year!" Gibson blurted.

Tennessee would not vote in favor of secession that January 9th, 1861. The state would have to wait until June before another vote would be taken. However, the State of South Carolina would pass a resolution to leave the Union, followed by six other Southern states. For the remainder of the weekend, the guests and household of Willow Ashby would celebrate the Christmas holiday in safety and plenty. The years of unhappiness that Cordelia had felt growing up without the love of her father had slowly begun to be replaced with a sense of devotion that was shared between niece and aunt.

Between Christmas and New Year's, Willow gave a grand ball at her home. Simon and Gibson were dressed in their cadet uniforms, both looking dashing in their military attire. Louise had fashioned a lovely ball gown for Cordelia in pink tarleton. The dress featured a double skirt; the upper one looped up with large bows of black velvet ribbon. The body was made round at the bottom, and was finished with a draping of folds at the top. The sleeve consisted of a broad fold of the tarleton, plaited into the armhole, surmounted by an epaulette in black velvet. It was a work of art, and Cordelia had never owned a more beautiful gown. Martha curled Cordelia's long brown locks in the sausage curls popular in young ladies of her age group. She wore a wreath of deep burgundy and pink rose buds. Willow had let her borrow the garnet earbobs that she had received from her own mother upon her marriage to Elijah Ashby.

The young guests began arriving before eight o'clock. The third floor had been transformed into a grand ballroom, equipped with a polished dance floor and lovely chandelier that was made especially for the height of the ceiling in the attic. Cordelia received guests as the co-hostess for the event. How Cordelia wished her best friend, Anna Mosby, had been able to attend the event. The young belle had hosted her own Christmas event, so it was promised that she would make the trip as soon as the weather was more agreeable to traveling by carriage.

The servants made several trips up the two flights of stairs to the ballroom, carrying trays of refreshments for the young people. Willow was matronly fashionable in a dark burgundy taffeta ball gown. As she circulated among the guests, Gibson asked for a dance with Cordelia. The two made a handsome couple on the dance floor, both having learned the dance steps to the Virginia Reel. After filling her dance card with several young gentlemen, Cordelia finished the last dance of the ball with Gibson.

Simon Ashby had not chosen a favorite young lady with whom to share the majority of his dances. He instead made it a point to dance with a different young lady for each. At the end of the evening, Gibson escorted Cordelia back downstairs to the formal parlor.

"I had no idea you were such an excellent dancer, Miss Cordelia. I hope I didn't step on your toes too many times during the evening," Gibson pronounced, giving a devilish smile.

"You dance marvelously, Gibson. I've enjoyed having the opportunity to talk with you at length over the past week," Cordelia remarked.

"Thank you, Miss Cordelia. It would please me greatly to have the opportunity to see you again, if you would allow it," Gibson asked, hoping for a favorable reply.

Cordelia blushed, this being her first beau, or the prospect of one. She raised her eyes to meet Gibson's. "I would very much like the opportunity to see you again, Gibson."

The two continued their conversation while Willow and Simon spoke quietly across the room. Soon, both Gibson and Simon would be reporting back to Nashville to the Military Academy. In a short time the country would spiral into Civil War, and the innocence of this time in their lives would be forever lost.

Chapter 19

APRIL, 1861

Tennessee would be the last of the Confederate states to secede from the Union. In all, 11 states formed the Confederate States of America. With the firing on Fort Sumter, President Abraham Lincoln began making plans to invade the South with an army of some 75,000 volunteers. Southern homes and hearths were all touched by the coming invasion, many rushing to the local courthouses and parade grounds to muster into service for The Cause.

Simon Ashby, Gibson Hughes, and the other cadets of the Western Military Academy were no exception. Under the direction of Col. Bushrod Johnson, many of the young men rushed out to sign their enlistment papers. Those too young to enlist found ways to join a local regiment before all the excitement would be over. Simon and Gibson, along with another cadet, Sam Davis, left the Academy that summer expecting to return in the fall, the war over and the South the victor. On the 9th of May, Gibson Hughes enlisted with the 1st Tennessee Infantry Regiment at Nashville, Tennessee, in Company A, the Rock City Guards. Simon Ashby went back to his home in Columbia, where he enlisted in Company H with the Maury Grays.

As soon as word reached Cordelia that Gibson Hughes had signed his papers, she asked if he might make a visit to Columbia before mustering into service. Gibson would make one last trip to his mother's plantation home in Goodlettsville, then would join Simon and his family before reporting to Nashville. Finally, in June, the vote was taken in favor of Tennessee separating from the Union to join the Southern Confederacy. The city of Nashville became a hotbed of activity, preparing to support the impending war effort.

The city of Columbia, Tennessee, was like other towns throughout the South. Patriotism was strong in the hearts of its citizens. Willow found herself remembering another war, in 1847. Emma and Simon were small children, and Willow was left to handle the plantation house near Spring Hill alone while her husband, Elijah, heeded the call of President Polk to go to Mexico. She would have to prepare herself for her young son to join with the country's lifeblood to defend their families and homes from the Yankee invaders.

It was decided that Willow would help to organize the local women in getting supplies gathered from the families in the town. Places were secured that could be used as hospitals, when the need would arise. Presently, several ladies from the community had gathered at the home of Willow Ashby to sew a battle flag for the local regiment. Across the hall from her room, Cordelia saw Simon looking out his window at the activity in the street below. Cordelia walked across the hallway and stuck her head inside the doorway of his room.

"How many kisses did you get today from all the Athenaeum girls?" she asked in a teasing manner.

Simon blushed, then said, "I got a couple of hankies, but no kisses."

Cordelia smiled. She had come to enjoy the ease with which she and Simon could talk. He had become more like her brother in the year that she had been with Willow. Now, she would have to see him off with the regiment of young men from the county. Another soldier was weighing on her mind as well.

"Aunt Willow said that we will go to Nashville to see you and Gibson off. I had hoped he could come here for a short visit," Cordelia remarked, sounding disappointed.

Simon finished packing his bag, then replied, "We are going to thrash those Yankees, Cordie. Everyone knows a Southerner can whip any Yankee."

Cordelia forced a smile, then gave Simon a hug. He tensed, then relaxed. He had only been hugged by Martha and his Mother. He allowed his cousin this moment of affection.

"It's not like I won't be back, Cordie. Come on, help me carry my things downstairs. We'll have to leave soon."

Later that afternoon, the two gray mares were hitched to the carriage by Cyrus and Jethro. The house servants had gathered in the front parlor where Willow had prepared to give Simon his father's two Colt revolver pistols, bullet mold, accoutrements and sword. She wished he could be here to present them to his son. Martha wiped her eyes as Simon bent to embrace his mother.

"Thank you, Mother. I'll take good care of the pistols. No other soldier will have such fine pieces as these," Simon appraised proudly.

Louise brought forth a small flag that she had lovingly crafted, the offering of which caused Simon to clear his throat before he spoke.

"Thank you, Louise. I'll make sure it doesn't get any holes in it," he said, bending down to embrace the petite servant.

Simon's uniform consisted of a gray frock coat with dark blue cuffs, and a pair of wool pants with a dark blue stripe down the leg. His gray kepi had the brass insignia of the company in the center of the hat. He promised to have a photograph taken upon arriving in Nashville, to be sent back to Willow. On this day, Simon Ashby would be leaving Columbia with his regiment, each of the young men full of promise in the prime of their youth. Tennessee would offer up its lifeblood in defense of the Confederacy.

Willow and Cordelia would travel to Nashville to join with others in the city to wish the men well as they marched to Camp Harris, near Franklin County. Upon arriving in the city, Willow accompanied Cordelia to the square where Gibson Hughes had been drilling since early April. The regiment was in the process of forming rank, and Cordelia caught her first glimpse of Gibson since Christmas. He made his way over to her, taking off his cap.

"Miss Cordie! Mrs. Ashby! I was afraid I wouldn't see you before we mustered out today!" Gibson exclaimed.

Cordelia admired the way Gibson filled out his uniform, and she wanted to have a memory of him on this day.

"Mr. Hughes, you look quite handsome in your uniform. I feel such pride in our soldiers. Simon is with his regiment near the parade ground. Would there be time to walk with us?" Willow asked, hoping to give the two time to talk.

Gibson smiled from ear to ear, extending one arm for Cordelia and the other for Willow. The three walked towards the parade grounds where several more regiments were now forming.

"Miss Cordie, I wasn't sure you would be able to make the trip, so I took the liberty of sending you a photograph. I hope it wasn't too forward of me," Gibson shyly commented.

Willow unleashed her arm, falling behind the two, but at the expected distance of a chaperone. The couple hadn't noticed.

"Thank you, Gibson. How thoughtful of you. If you would like, I could have a photograph made for you today. I could send it to you, if you'd like?" Cordelia offered.

Gibson and Cordelia continued talking, until they found the Maury Grays. Simon spotted the trio first, waving his hand to get their attention.

"Aunt Willow, I see Simon!" Cordelia happily announced.

Gibson and Simon shook hands, commenting on the attire and accoutrements of the other. Willow was particularly happy that the two would be part of the same regiment. As they continued to talk, a bugle was sounded, and both young soldiers knew it was time to fall in with their respective regiments. Cordelia hugged her cousin, and this time Simon reciprocated happily. He embraced his mother, breathing in her rose water perfume. She took his face in her hands, not caring it wasn't proper to show such emotion in public. She kissed his cheek, a tear trailing down her cheek.

"God go with you, son. I'll be praying for you and all the boys," Willow said, her voice quavering with emotion.

"I'll be home before you know it, Mother. Write to me as soon as I give you an address. I'll be waiting for word from you about everyone."

After another quick embrace, Simon ran off to join his regiment. Cordelia, Willow, and Gibson made their way back to the square where the Rock City Guards were forming. Before Gibson parted company, he bent down to hug Willow.

"Thank you for coming, Mrs. Ashby. If something happens to me, I would rest knowing you are looking after Miss Cordie. You're all she has," he said softly.

He turned to Cordelia and gave her a quick embrace. It took her by surprise, but she liked the feeling of his arms around her.

"I'll be looking forward to receiving that photograph of you, Miss Cordie."

"I will go as soon as we leave today, Gibson. Please take care of yourself!" Cordelia admonished.

The band began to play "Dixie," a very popular new song. Soon, the 1,250 men marched toward the train station amid the cheers and kisses of adoring ladies. As they passed the Masonic Hall, each member of the regiment was given a bouquet of flowers by the ladies from the Soldiers Friend Society. Boarding railcars, the 1st Tennessee would make their way to Allisonia, Tennessee, on the Nashville and Chattanooga railroad. After a few weeks of training at Camp Harris, the regiment would move to Camp Cheatham in Robertson County. It was here that the men would begin their training in earnest. They would receive thorough training in Hardee's tactics and two daily drills. But in addition to the rigors of drilling and marching, they would spend the next month fighting two unseen enemies: disease and illness. The regiment would be reduced to 944 men. While at Camp Cheatham, the men made a trip as a regiment into Goodlettsville, the home of Gibson Hughes, to vote on the question of secession on June 22. Gibson's mother, Fannie Hughes, and his mammy, Aunt Beck, would bring gifts of two new shirts and three pair of breeches for their young soldier.

Upon their return to Camp Cheatham, the boys of the 1st Tennessee would receive a visit from the ladies of the Nashville Female Academy. The graduating class presented a Regimental flag to the men. For many of the soldiers the time spent at Camp Cheatham seemed interminably long, as they were fervently hoping to see fighting. They would soon get their wish, as word came to the 1st Tennessee that they would report to Virginia on July 10. Men hurriedly packed for the train ride back to Nashville.

It was from this camp that Cordelia and Willow would receive their first correspondence from Gibson and Simon since they marched away on May 10, 1861.

Chapter 20

Willow Ashby didn't waste time joining with others in the war effort. Not long after the 1st Tennessee Infantry marched out of Nashville, the women of Columbia stepped into action for the Cause. Willow had Louise and Martha assemble a sewing room in the front parlor. Several of the ladies in the St. Peter's Episcopal Church had their husbands and servants bring their sewing machines to Willow's house on West 7th Street. That summer would be a busy time for Cordelia and her aunt, sewing underwear and shirts for the boys from Maury County. Cordelia would also include homemade items for Gibson Hughes.

In addition to the shirts and underwear, the servants stayed busy rolling bandages from the cotton cloth that had been donated, while others began knitting socks that would undoubtedly be a much desired item when the war dragged on into winter. The ladies came after lunch, staying until late in the afternoon. The warm days and crowded room didn't diminish the zeal with which the women performed their tasks.

"Miz Willow, de postman came early this mornin'," announced Louise, as she entered into the dining room where Cordelia and Willow were eating their breakfast.

"Thank you, Louise. You may leave it on the table," Willow instructed.

Cordelia had been anxiously awaiting news from Simon and Gibson, and this morning her waiting would come to an end. Cordelia finished breakfast in a more determined manner, eyeing the two envelopes on the table. Willow tried to remain more sedate as she finished with the last morsels of eggs and ham. Both women waited for Martha to remove the plates from the table, then Willow reached for the two envelopes. The first, addressed to Cordelia, was passed to her to read in private. Willow opened the letter from Simon slowly, closing her eyes in a prayer of thanksgiving for even this smallest of blessings.

Willow noticed the date of the letter to be almost two weeks prior, June 22, 1861. She looked up at Cordelia, who hadn't yet begun to read her letter. Cordelia put the letter on her lap, waiting for her aunt to tell her the contents of Simon's letter.

"He says that the train ride to Camp Cheatham came only a few days after they arrived at Camp Harris." The news surprised Cordelia, but she listened as her aunt continued. "The boys made a trip into Goodlettsville to vote for secession, where Simon says Mrs. Hughes and a servant came into town with gifts. He also tells about the sickness they have encountered in just a short time. Oh, he says that Gibson's brigade had an outbreak of dysentery."

Again, Cordelia was concerned, anxious to open her letter.

"Simon said they drill most of the day, but he would rather be fighting the Yankees," Willow relayed, a tone of apprehension in her otherwise soft voice.

Willow finished by saying that the whole regiment was waiting for action, but if possible, could there be a package soon of some of Martha's biscuits and apple butter. Cordelia smiled, knowing that her cousin was quite fond of Martha's extra portions for her favorite. Wrapped neatly in the letter was a small case, something Willow was anxiously opening. A small tintype of Simon, taken while in Nashville that May, showed a young man of 18, full of life and promise. Willow held it to her breast, as if the recipient of his very essence.

"He looks so handsome, Aunt Willow. I never noticed before, but I see a resemblance in our features. Perhaps it is our eyes?"

Willow noticed, and commented, "Would you like to read your letter from Mr. Hughes in private?"

Cordelia could feel a small picture in her envelope as well. She slowly unwrapped the contents, revealing a similar pose of Gibson Hughes. She handed the small black case to her aunt.

"He looks very gallant in his uniform, Cordelia. We must place these on the mantel so that we can give them their place of honor."

Cordelia agreed, but asked if she could keep the picture in her room, for now, as she read her letter from Gibson. She excused herself, taking the letter up to her bedroom where she could read the contents in private.

June 25th, 1861 ~ Camp Cheatham, Tennessee

Dear Miss Cordie,

I take pen in hand to give you a brief account of my days since arriving here a few weeks ago. The days are filled with learning tactics, marching and forming lines. A few days prior, I had the pleasure of seeing my dear mother and mammy, Aunt Beck. Our whole regiment rode the train into Goodlettsville. I was bestowed new pants and shirts. Aunt Beck brought one of her molasses cakes, which I was inclined to hide for my own, but shared with my pards.

I have thought of you often, and I hope you are well. Please tell Mrs. Ashby hello, and if you have occasion to speak with Miss Mosby, pass along that I have heard her brothers', Jed's and Joel's, names mentioned as part of Company D. I believe they went by the name Williamson Grays. Now we're all part of the same. It seems queer that just a year ago we would make acquaintance when they brought you to Columbia.

I hope the photograph will arrive without damage. I would surely be honored to carry a likeness of you with me into battle. I will write again when I am more sure of where we will be.

Your friend,
Gibson Hughes
Pvt. 1st Tennessee

Cordelia read the letter again, clinging to each word. Finally, she carefully folded the stationery and placed it back in the envelope. Walking to her dressing table, she lifted the lid to a small sewing basket where she kept her personal belongings. It was there that she placed his letter. As directed, she began to pen a letter to her dear friend, Anna Mosby, of Franklin. She would relay the message of Gibson in regard to the brothers. She also invited her to come for an extended visit. Perhaps the two could comfort each other with their loved ones away answering the call of duty.

On July 10, the regiment of the 1st Tennessee reached Nashville. The ladies of the Nashville Academy entertained the men on the grounds of their school that evening. The following morning, throngs of well-wishers flocked to the city to give the regiment a warm welcome. The Rock City Guards, along with the other regiments that had joined with them, boarded railcars for Virginia. Word of their brief stay in Nashville reached Willow and Cordelia too late to make the trip. Cordelia did manage to send a carte de visite to Gibson, and it would be with him when he left that July day.

Word seemed to travel slowly for Cordelia and Willow. Each afternoon, Willow sent Jethro to purchase a newspaper, hoping to keep abreast of war news. Perhaps having a premonition of times that were to come, Willow instructed the servants to prepare a larger garden. In the early morning, she and Cordelia donned their work dresses and joined in with the servants to pull weeds in the back garden. Never before had Cordelia performed such an arduous task. However, food might be scarce if the war dragged on through the winter.

From the pulpit to the sewing circle, most conversations began and ended with "the war." It was ever present in the minds of all Southerners, and now the Yankees had invaded Virginia. Jethro had brought the news that July afternoon, word of a battle at Manassas Junction, a routing by the Confederate Army. Along with the news, came the first of many casualty lists that would accompany the war commentary.

Willow gathered everyone in the front parlor and read the account of the Sunday afternoon battle. A Virginian by the name of Thomas Jackson became the hero of the battle. The paper gave him the new name of "Stonewall" following his heroic stand. The servants of Willow Ashby listened intently for any word of the boys from the 1st Tennessee, but apparently they were not part of the fray.

Cordelia was happy to receive word that her dear friend, Anna Mosby, would be arriving in late July to spend the rest of the summer with her in Columbia. Anna arrived on the 27th of July with her mother, Jennie Mosby. Anna's father felt a trip south might offer Jennie a brief respite from the ever present worry of her two sons off fighting in Virginia. Willow welcomed Mrs. Mosby, Anna, and Bess, their servant, to her home. The servants carried several large trunks up the impressive flight of stairs to the guest rooms above. As Martha directed the ladies to the rooms they would occupy, Louise and Bess took to putting their personal effects and articles of clothing into the large standing wardrobes in each of their rooms. After this task was completed, Willow suggested the ladies rest while dinner was prepared. Bess left her mistress and accompanied Martha to the summer kitchen where Esther had begun a meal of fried chicken, dumplings and roasting ears.

Cordelia found it hard to rest on this warm afternoon. She opened the window as wide as she could, hoping to feel some relief. Reclining on the bed, she draped her arm over her eyes to block out the sunlight. As she drifted off to sleep, the faces of Pharaoh, Mammy Cilla, and her childhood playmates filled her subconscious thoughts. She heard the song that she had heard so often from the row of cabins behind the cedar thicket. *There is a balm in Gilead, to make the wounded whole, there is a balm in Gilead, to heal the sin sick soul...* The sweet voices lulled Cordelia to sleep. When she awoke, the cruel face of Lucas Crenshaw was still in her memory. His black eyes reminded her of the devil himself. The pain she felt that day in Pharaoh and Mammy Cilla's cabin was still fresh, and the tears flowed from her eyes and puddled in her ears.

Cordelia sat up quickly, the sound of Willow's shoes on the wooden floor in the wide hall startling her.

"Dear, are you all right? I thought I heard you crying," Willow softly inquired. She came into the room, sitting beside Cordelia on the bed. Cordelia quickly wiped the tears from her face.

"I had a nightmare, Aunt Willow. I was at Fairview, listening to Mammy Cilla and the others singing like always. Then when I opened the cabin door to listen, Crenshaw was there, like before," Cordelia sobbed.

Willow pulled a small handkerchief from her sleeve, handing it to Cordelia.

"My dear, it was appalling what the overseer said to you. It was cruel and hurtful for him to relish your pain. But what's done is done."

She would never forget her father's servants, and she wouldn't rest until she knew where Pharaoh, Mammy Cilla, and Nancy were sold.

"Thank you for listening, Aunt Willow."

Cordelia followed Willow downstairs, where dinner would soon be served. Willow became better acquainted with Mrs. Mosby during dinner. She asked about Joel, whom she remembered fondly. She inquired about the older son, Jed, listening intently as Mrs. Mosby shared about his recent engagement to a young belle from Franklin. Later that evening, the houseguests donned their shawls and accompanied Willow and Cordelia on an evening stroll. Jennie Mosby found the homes lovely, and the citizens she met quite charming.

The following morning, Martha carried a tray out to the carriage house where Jethro and Cyrus were changing the shoes on Willow Ashby's prized gray mares. She entered the structure silently, and the two men were obviously unaware they had company.

"Now you watch, ol' Yankee boys'll be settin' all de' slaves free as sho' as Jesus!" Cyrus commented, sure that his days of servitude were almost over.

Jethro stopped his hammering. "Jes' whats you thinkin' the Yankees care one spit in de wind about us darkies?" he retorted smugly.

Martha cleared her throat, making her presence known. The two stopped their conversing and smiled at the jug of water Martha was toting.

"Neither of you gots any worries 'bout the Yankees coming into Columbia. We's slaves, always has been, always will be."

The men took the cups from Martha, wiping the sweat from their faces with their shirts. The heat was already becoming a bother on this warm July day.

"You goin' to the post today , Jethro?" Martha asked.

"Miz Willow and Miz Cordie wants to mail de letters to Massa' Simon and that beau of Miz Cordie's. I 'spect the Mosby's have letters too," Jethro presumed.

"I hope Massa Simon's all right. I heard de mournin' dove outside three nights in a row. I'm sho' Miz Willow heard it too," Martha shared, trying to keep her voice low.

"Lewis say they is somewhere o'er in Virginny. Ol' Massa 's pistols might get a firin' yet!" Jethro said with a laugh.

Martha didn't like his tone, as she was genuinely concerned for Simon. She had been his nurse since he was a newborn. Jethro and Cyrus finished their drinks, then went back to work. Martha took the tray back in the kitchen where Esther was finishing kneading a pile of dough. Esther closed the door, a sign that she had something important to share with Martha.

"What you closing the door fo?" Martha asked, clearly perturbed from the lack of a breeze.

"I overheerd Cyrus talkin' to Jethro when they's out in de garden. He say he gonna run north, jest as soon as de Yankees come," Esther shared, her voice taking on a secretive tone.

"After Miz Willow took him in an' give him a good home? What's he think he doin'? Jus' run an git hisself killed is what he be doin," Martha scoffed.

"Me and Jethro don't have no place to go, Martha. We be stayin' on with Miz Willow. She's a good woman, even if she *is* white."

Sunday morning meant church services for all at Willow Ashby's residence. Following an early breakfast, Bess had been summoned to help her mistresses dress for the day. Martha and Louise were helping Willow and Cordelia with their morning toiletries. All of the servants were expected to don their Sunday best to attend services at St. Peter's Episcopal Church across the street. They would take their place in the back row of pews.

While the Mosby ladies and Bess visited Willow Ashby's home, they gave the servants the latest news from near Nashville. Martha especially enjoyed accompanying her mistress to Nashville. She remembered their most recent visit, watching the slaves being loaded into buckboard wagons and taken from the warehouse. She remembered being separated from her mother and father when Willow left Dryer Hall and married Elijah Ashby. She had been only 18 years of age. She swore an oath that very day that she would never marry or bring a child into the world of slavery.

Her loyalty to Willow was evident in the secrets the two had shared over the years that had remained between them. One secret would soon come to light, and the lives of those Willow loved the most in this world would be affected.

August came and the dog days of summer were particularly bothersome. The slaves worked in the garden behind Willow's home early in the morning to avoid the heat of the day. Cyrus continued to listen to talk among the other slaves he had met while at the livery stable behind the post office. Anna and Cordelia grew closer than sisters that first summer of the war. The young women spent a good deal of time knitting socks and making scarves and mittens to send to Simon, Gibson, and Anna's beau, Sam Walker. Both girls had been fortunate to receive photographs of their beaus on the day of their mustering.

Cordelia and Anna wrote weekly to their soldier beaus and Simon. Worry began to set in when a month had passed and no letters arrived. Jennie and Willow shared the unspoken fear that had been plaguing their thoughts one morning at breakfast.

"I don't know why we haven't received any word from the boys..."

Willow remembered the early days of the Mexican War, when her own dear husband was away fighting near Vera Cruz. It was the plight of all wives and sweethearts to fret over the safety of their soldiers so far from home and hearth. Now, she tried to remain the voice of calm.

"Mrs. Mosby, I do believe there is a good reason for the delay in response from our sons. I'm sure we'll receive word soon," came the soft-spoken reply from Willow.

The two women continued their breakfast while Anna and Cordelia organized boxes of supplies to be sent to soldiers in the front parlor. The sewing machines were quiet this morning, as the heat had fatigued several of the older matrons who had faithfully labored for days finishing several pairs of new uniform pants that were to be sent to the Maury Grays. Louise, Bess, and Esther finished folding the shirts that were sewn that morning.

The sound of the back door closing went unnoticed, and Jethro came into the house, removing his cap as he entered the dining room.

"Beg pardon, Miz Willow. I's brung de mail," Jethro said, waiting for Willow to acknowledge him.

Willow and Jennie, almost forgetting their good breeding, lunged for the mail that was in Jethro's dark, leathery hands. Willow thanked Jethro, taking the mail and quickly looking through the stack that was bound together with a string.

"Mrs. Mosby, I believe we have quite a cache of correspondence today!" she declared with a girlish lilt in her voice.

Jennie Mosby felt sure her heart was dangerously close to beating through her chest with the anticipation of what the large stack of mail could mean. Willow carefully looked at each postmark. Seven letters were neatly placed in the stack that came from the Columbia Post Office. Two letters were addressed to Miss Cordelia Barlow, two letters were for Mrs. Elijah Ashby, two letters for Mrs. Evan Mosby, and one letter was addressed to Miss Anna Mosby. As Willow sifted through the rest of the mail, she noticed two other envelopes. A letter from the Nashville Hotel was addressed to Cordelia, and a letter from Evan Mosby to his wife was the final piece of mail. Willow rang a dainty silver bell that sat on the mantel above the fireplace. In a matter of seconds, Martha and Bess appeared from the central hallway.

"Yas'm, Miz Willow?" Martha asked, entering the room.

"Martha, please tell Miss Cordelia and Miss Anna that the post has been delivered," Willow instructed.

As Martha left with the mail, Bess attended to her mistress.

"Miss Jennie, would you like your reading spectacles?"

Jennie Mosby was accustomed to Bess attending to her needs without giving it a passing thought, but today she made a point of thanking her.

"Why yes, I would. Thank you, Bess," she said sincerely.

Willow wanted to retire to the coolness of her bedroom in the rear of the home. She wanted to read Simon's letters in private. Not wanting to offend her guest, Willow remained with Jennie until Bess returned with her eyeglasses. Jennie excused herself to the confines of her bedroom.

Willow dismissed Lewis, not needing his services the rest of the morning. She closed the door to her bedroom and slowly read the first of her two letters. The envelope had a postmark of July 25, a month prior.

July 25th, 1861 ~ Virginia

Dear Mother,

I received your letter before we left for Virginia. Please thank Martha for the preserves. I shared with my mess mates, and they claimed their own mamas could hardly do better. We came to Virginia on the railroad, hoping to meet the Yankees at Manassas Junction. We didn't get to take part in the battle. Mother, you should see the wild hoopdeedoo that's all about. It's a sight to see. But there are many who were shot in battle; such a pitiful lot they are. I am most anxious to shoot Father's pistols. We are moving out today. The Colonel says Staunton, Virginia. I will write when we make camp. Tell Cordie I saw Gibson. If the war ends before winter, we should be home by Christmas.

Your loving son, Simon

Willow laid the letter on the bed, then quickly opened the next envelope. The next letter was a bit longer, telling of the arrival at Staunton, Virginia. Willow didn't get the complete version of life as an 18-year-old soldier, but the descriptions of camp life that Simon did share were interesting to Willow. Simon and his friend, Dooley Eldridge, had their first taste of Virginia whiskey. It was also in this quaint little town where Simon developed a tolerance for the taste of good "Virginny baccy," as Dooley called it.

Willow tried to imagine the clutter of so many men in such small confines. Simon described the town as best he could. They visited the houses for the insane and blind, something all the soldiers wanted to see. Unknown to Willow, her son also became schooled in the games of chance and gambling. Simon was a quick study, and soon had made a nice bundle from his pards. Before ending his letter, he described a march up the Allegheny Mountains. He didn't go into great detail. Willow was thankful that her son was safe and, from his tone, would be marching back to Columbia before Christmas. She quickly set about writing of the latest news in town.

Martha deposited the letters addressed to Cordelia and Anna, leaving the two young women giggling with delight. Each sat in one of the large Queen Anne chairs that flanked the bay window. A slight breeze blew the draperies that hung in the bay window as the envelopes were opened. The neatly folded paper fluttered as Cordelia removed her first letter. The Nashville Hotel letter took second precedence to the letters from Gibson Hughes. With shaking hands, Cordelia took a deep breath, then began to silently read her first letter.

11 August, 1861 ~ Valley Mountain

Dear Miss Cordie,
I was surprised to get three letters in the post delivery yesterday. I am looking forward to getting the new pants and shirts. Please give my thanks to the ladies in your sewing circle. I want to tell you now what camp life is like here. We arrived in Manassas Junction the night the Yankee army got a walloping. We soon got our marching orders. We are in Valley Mountain, and it is much nicer here. The 7th Tennessee and the 14th Tennessee have joined us. We have a new captain; Henry Webster was elected. Some of the boys have been partaking in spirits and tobacco. I find both distasteful. I have found myself in a game of cards now and then, but the only winnings have been a pocket watch. Oh, the boredom that consumes most of the day. Night before last, I was put on picket duty. I haven't even fired my gun at a Yankee yet. Have you had any balls in Mrs. Ashby's ballroom? I want to hear news of your days, and what the goings on are at home. Please tell Martha, Mrs. Ashby, and the Mosby ladies hello for me.

I remain your admirer and friend,
Gibson Hughes

Cordelia finished the letter, placing it back in its envelope. She glanced over at Anna, who was reading the second page of her letter. Cordelia waited until she finished.

"How is Sam, Anna?" Cordelia inquired.

Anna carefully placed the letter back in the small envelope.

"Sam is doing fine. He said he spent a whole day digging a ditch for the privy. He and his brother, Joseph, found a pig wandering around camp. They have had quite a feast! I hope he gets to come home for Christmas."

Jennie Mosby's letter was an urgent plea from her husband to bring their daughter and come home to Oak Hill. Evan Mosby would be joining others who felt the patriot call after the battle of Manassas Junction. Jennie summoned Bess to begin packing their trunks. Willow Ashby's guests would be leaving the following day for Franklin.

Cordelia had forgotten the letter from the Nashville Hotel until later the following afternoon when she returned from the train depot. She had finished her lunch with Willow, then retired to her bedroom for the rest of the afternoon to write letters to Gibson and Simon. It was then that she noticed she had not opened the third letter.

The letter was to inform Cordelia that her stepmother, Rachel, had remarried and left Nashville. She instructed the management at the hotel to contact Cordelia, requesting that she come to collect all the personal papers and family items belonging to her deceased father.

For a moment, Cordelia sat in disbelief. How quickly her stepmother had found another husband. The letter shared that the items would be kept in storage for a time, but she would have to make the trip to Nashville within a few days. She found her aunt in the garden. She had come to love Willow, and she wanted to seek her advice.

"Aunt Willow, I received a letter from the Nashville Hotel. My stepmother has remarried. It appears that she left all of my father's personal papers and personal property. The hotel is requesting that I come to Nashville to retrieve the items," Cordelia pronounced.

Willow noticed the apprehension in Cordelia's voice. She set her basket on the bench and took Cordelia's hand.

"Cordelia, I will go with you, if you would like."

She put her arms around Willow, thanking her aunt. Cordelia was thankful that she would not have to make the trip to Nashville alone.

After her discussion about the letter with Willow, the two retired to their rooms for the evening. Cordelia changed quickly, donning her cotton nightgown. She left the lamp burning on her bedside table, unable to stop the thoughts going through her mind. Perhaps the name of the person who bought Pharaoh, Mammy Cilla, and the other servants would be somewhere in the papers. She found herself looking at the portrait of her mother, above the fireplace mantle. Studying the portrait, she could now see the resemblance of her Aunt Willow with her mother. The same line of the cheek, small mouth, and deep-set eyes was shared by her cousin, Simon. Her thoughts traveled to her days on the cool cabin floor of Mammy Cilla, and carefree afternoons listening to the songs being sung under the ash tree by the slaves; a particular song now repeated in her dream. That night, after the lamp's fire was extinguished, the words of the song haunted her slumber. *Nora, Nora, let me come in, the doors are fastened and the windows pinned, keep your hands on that plow, hold on....*Cordelia went from cabin to cabin searching for Mammy Cilla, but each cabin was empty.

Simon Ashby, Dooley Eldridge, and the rest of Company H of the 1st Tennessee had made camp near Big Springs, Virginia. War had seemed romantic to these 18-year-old boys. Since making their way from Bath Alum, the constant marching had taking its toll on the young recruits. An unexpected visitor made a lasting impression on the men of the 1st Tennessee. General Robert E. Lee arrived at camp, giving the young soldiers a glimpse of the great man. Simon wrote to his mother that very night about seeing the general, and how he reminded him of one of the deacons at church. His eyes were like that of a dove, and the softness of his voice made Simon wish he could have gotten to spend time just talking with him. His dress was impeccable, and Simon noticed General Lee had no weapon on his person, nor did he have an aide to accompany him. His larger-than-life presence within the camp was brief, but it was a morale boost for these young men so far from hearth and home.

Cordelia awoke the next morning drained from the previous night's restless slumber. She awoke later than she wanted, and now she had to hurry in order to get to the depot before the train pulled out of the station. Cordelia and Willow, along with Martha, boarded a train for Nashville the following day. When the train reached the depot in Nashville, the threesome found a carriage that would take them to the hotel. The weather had taken a turn, and a storm seemed to be brewing in the west. The desk clerk smiled and welcomed the ladies into the hotel.

"Would you ladies be needing a room?" the clerk inquired.

Willow approached the desk, making their introductions. "My name is Mrs. Elijah Ashby, and this is my niece, Miss Cordelia Barlow," Willow announced.

The clerk recognized the name, Barlow.

"Begging your pardon, Ma'am, but would you be Judge Barlow's daughter? We've been expecting you," the clerk said, smiling at Cordelia.

Willow spoke for Cordelia. "Yes, she would. She was summoned here today to retrieve her father's personal effects." The clerk suddenly felt as though his nose was being tweaked. Quickly, his professionalism returned.

"Of course. Please wait here," the young clerk requested, and disappeared to a small room behind the desk. Within a few seconds, the clerk returned with an older gentleman, pulling a medium-sized trunk. "Miss Barlow, your stepmother left this for you when she departed a week ago," the older gentleman said.

He pointed to the room and continued, "There are four crates in the storage room. We won't be able to continue storing them. We didn't know what else to do with them, Ma'am."

Willow instructed the clerk to send the crates and the trunk to her home in Columbia. She paid the clerk for the cost of shipping the items, then thanked the gentleman for taking care of the matter. Cordelia also thanked the gentleman and followed her aunt out the door.

"Is there anything else you would like to do while we are here, dear?" Willow asked.

Cordelia thought for a moment, then asked if they would have time to visit the Female Academy. She wanted to call on Mrs. Sturgeon. Before they made their way to the train station, they asked the carriage driver to make a stop at the Nashville Female Academy.

Chapter 23

The train ride back to Columbia gave Cordelia time to ponder what possessions of her father's were housed in the collection of crates. There were undoubtedly law books and papers amassed from Absalom Barlow's tenure as a lawyer and later, a judge, in Sumner and Robertson Counties. She decided that when Gibson Hughes returned from the war, she would present her father's law collection to him, since her father thought so highly of him. Willow wasn't sure why she felt the contents in the crates foretold more pain for Cordelia.

Cordelia wished there was time to stop in Franklin to check on the Mosbys. She wished Anna and her mother could have remained for a longer visit. It had been most pleasurable for Cordelia to have her closest friend near to share secrets with.

Upon arriving in Columbia, Willow spied her young slave, Cyrus, standing behind the dry goods store with two other Negro servants of Mr. Simpson, owner of Simpon's Dry Goods. She knew he couldn't have foreseen their arrival at the exact time, and his being away from her home and his chores bothered her.

Before she could approach him, her attention was drawn to a couple standing in front of the post office. It appeared to be bad news, although she couldn't tell for whom or what was the matter. She immediately recognized the pair and turned to her servant,

"Martha, wait with Miss Cordelia. I must go see what the matter is."

Willow Ashby saw the face of her dear friend, Mrs. Kate Caldwell. As she approached the woman, she saw a piece of paper in her hand and the ghostly white pallor of her face. Kate looked at Willow, appearing to be in a state of shock.

"Oh Kate, what is it?" Willow said softly, putting her arm around her friend.

"It's our boy, Will. Letter said he was shot in an ambush near Big Springs, Virginia. The letter is from a Captain Field."

Dr. Adolphus Caldwell tried to hold back the grief he was feeling, to comfort his wife, but the tears flowed as the blood flowed from his only son there on that mountain road in Virginia. Willow thought of her own son, Simon, who was part of Will's company. Perhaps she too had a letter waiting for her at home. Trying to put that thought from her mind, she summoned Martha to come to her.

"Martha, take Miss Cordelia home and tell Cyrus to get the wagon and Jethro. They will need to fetch the crates and trunk from the depot."

Cordelia saw the look of despair on the faces of Dr. and Mrs. Caldwell, then saw the sorrow in her aunt.

"Aunt Willow, is there anything I can do?"

Willow patted the hand of her niece, her eyes showing the compassion Cordelia knew so well.

"Yes. Please have Esther and Louise set about making a meal for Dr. and Mrs. Caldwell. I am going to see them home."

The war had claimed one of Maury County's youngest. Will Caldwell had urged his parents to sign the papers, and reluctantly they assented. At just 17, Will mustered with Simon and the Maury Grays. Now preparations would be made to travel to Virginia to retrieve their only son's body. Captain Field had instructed where his body was hastily buried, and when safe, travel could commence. The Caldwells had only their cook, a maid, and Dr. Caldwell's manservant. Who would be given the task of making the journey to bring the boy home would have to be discussed.

After the house was placed in mourning, Willow went to the dry goods store for the dye needed to prepare the clothing for deep mourning. Too grief-stricken herself, Kate allowed Willow Ashby to receive the callers who had heard of her son's passing. Word traveled quickly, as theirs was the first of Columbia's gallant young men to fall to a Yankee bullet.

Cordelia hurried into the house, summoning the servants to begin the list of tasks set out by Willow. As soon as she had done as her aunt instructed, she went to the long bureau table in the hallway. There, in a neat stack, was the previous day's mail delivery. Her heart in her throat, she quickly leafed through the various correspondences that were addressed to her aunt. There, in the bottom of the stack, were two letters with Confederate insignia. She felt her knees sway and a wave of nausea overtook her. Backing up to the bench that lined the wall, she felt her knees give way and she sat with a thud.

The first letter was addressed to her aunt, so she placed it beside her. A second letter, addressed to *Miss Cordelia Barlow,* remained to be opened. Cordelia inhaled deeply, then slowly exhaled as she tore the end of the envelope open. *Thank you, Jesus!* She quickly recognized the handwriting to be Gibson's. The date was August 10th, 1861, and the lines were written with a pencil which seemed to have been dull at the point. Cordelia slowly read the words written by Gibson, wishing she could hear his voice instead.

10 August 1861 ~

Dear Miss Cordie,

I hope these lines find you well. I read your letter I received today. A letter came from my Mother that she was keeping a loaded gun under the bed. Aunt Beck is afraid the Yankees will get into Goodlettsville. I will try and answer your questions now. We have marched a good bit over the past few days. It is hard to carry my pack, haversack, bedroll and clothes. I don't believe this war is going to be over by Christmas. We have followed General Lee and Stonewall all over this great land, trying to catch old Rosie. Now I will tell you about a sad day. One of the boys from your own Columbia and a few others were caught unawares by a group of Yankee scum. They were fired on, but Captain Fields opened his gun on them. They buried that boy, Caldwell, I believe, in a grave off from camp. I suspect his poor Mother has learned about his passing by now. We haven't lost any of our boys to the ball and shot, but a sickness has taken its hold on many. I suspect they will get their marching papers for home. Most are chompin' at the bit to kill Federals, but not fit to fight or march. Miss Cordie, I have your picture in my hand as I write this. To see you again would surely bring enjoyment to this soldier. I hope you are as besotted with me as I am smitten with you. I will try to pen you more lines when we get more paper. Rations haven't arrived, and food isn't as plentiful. Thanks be to the kind Virginia ladies for sharing their food and vegetables with the likes of us.

I am forever your admirer,
Gibson Hughes

Cordelia closed her eyes, saying a prayer of thanksgiving for Gibson's safety. She wished he had made mention of Simon. He would be part of the same company as Will Caldwell. What if he too were part of the wounded or killed? She wished her Aunt Willow would return so she could read the letter that was lying beside her now. Cordelia knew Willow wouldn't leave her friend in her state of shock and grief. Long after evening prayers were said, Cordelia fell asleep on the settee in the front parlor. She once again dreamed of her days at Fairview. In this dream, the mournful sound of the slaves lifting their voices above the despondent parents of little Benny filled her ears. She recognized the melody from the many times she had laid on top of the quilted bed while Mammy Cilla, Nancy, and the other slave women sang around the fire, sewing scraps of material together in a large quilt. Now the song seemed to be sung by those who were standing over a body in repose. *There is a balm in Gilead, to make the wounded whole, there is a balm in Gilead, to heal the sin-sick soul...*As Cordelia walked closer, she saw the lean shape of a soldier in gray pants and frock coat, his wound-stained shirt crimson against his skin. It was then that the face became clear, and she recognized Gibson! The scream that rose from her throat woke her from the horrible dream.

"Miz Cordie, you's havin' a nightmare!" Martha said, gently shaking her shoulder.

Cordelia rubbed her eyes, relieved that it was only a dream. She smiled at Martha, whose face for a moment reminded her of Mammy Cilla.

"I'm all right, Martha. It was just a dream."

Cordelia wanted to ask Martha a question that had been on her mind for some time. "Martha, did you know my mother?"

Martha shook her head to confirm that she did. Cordelia continued, "I remember Pharaoh and Mammy Cilla saying they had been on my grandfather's plantation before they came to live with my parents. That means you knew them too."

"Yas'm, Miz Cordie. I know'd them. Pharaoh's own Ma was the Mammy to Miz Willow and Miz Lucretia," Martha shared.

Cordelia wished she had learned more of her mother and her grandparents. It was then that she remembered her father's belongings.

"Did Cyrus and Jethro fetch the crates like Aunt Willow asked?"

Martha was glad the subject had been changed. She acknowledged the crates were being stored out in the carriage house. The trunk had been placed on the third floor, in the now unused ballroom. Since the beginning of the war, it was once again an attic.

"Well, it's too late this evening to start on that. I think I will wait for Aunt Willow a little longer."

Martha started to walk out of the room, then added, "I done sent Jethro over to fetch Miz Willow. She can't do no mo' for the doctor and his wife now."

"Thank you, Martha. Good night," Cordelia softly replied.

Chapter 24

Willow closed the door, waking Cordelia. She put her shawl and bag on the table in the hall and, seeing Cordelia, smiled.

"You didn't have to wait up for me, dear," Willow said, her voice weary.

Cordelia walked over to the bench where she had left the letter that was addressed to Willow.

"I wanted to give you this, Aunt Willow," Cordelia said, holding out the envelope bearing the military insignia.

A look of trepidation enclosed Willow's face as she took the letter from Cordelia. She took it into the library, where she lit the lamp on the small table.

"I would like you to stay, Cordelia. I don't know if I dare read it."

Cordelia sat beside her aunt, who still had not opened the envelope.

"Would you like for me to read it, Aunt Willow? "

Willow handed the letter to Cordelia, who now nervously ripped open the outer envelope. With shaky hands, she opened the letter. At first, she felt as though her heart stopped beating. The letter was not in the hand of Simon Ashby, but another soldier. It was from Dooley Eldridge.

August ~

Deer Missus Ashby,

I rite to you sence Simon ain't fit to do it hisself. He come down with a case of the croop. We marched too days in rain and slop, now he is feverd. He ask me to anser his leter from you. If he is able, we march to Winchester at tomarros lite. He sends love to you and Mis Cordie.

Privet Dooley Eldridge

Cordelia shared the contents of the letter and, afterwards, the two women hugged over the joy of his just being sick. His infirmity was nothing trivial, but after the news that was received earlier that day about young Will Caldwell, they were thankful.

"Cordelia, we must send Jethro to fetch Will's body for the Caldwells. I don't think Dr. Caldwell wants to send Percy alone."

That evening, Cordelia lay awake until the wee hours of the morning. She couldn't help but worry about Simon, for his condition was serious. Perhaps he would be sent home? Willow began writing the necessary papers for Jethro to accompany Percy to retrieve the remains of the young Caldwell boy. One of the men from the Masonic Lodge, Mr. Blake Goodman, would offer his time and wagon to supervise the two on their mission.

The month of September would usher in a change for the residents of Nashville and the surrounding areas as war would come to Tennessee.

Chapter 25

General Albert Sidney Johnston would arrive in Nashville to take command of the Western Theater, with his headquarters across the Cumberland River at Edgefield. Much fanfare and excitement was reported in the newspapers in and around the city, with the residents of Columbia feeling the apprehension of Yankees crossing into their homeland.

Willow spent her days offering assistance to Dr. and Mrs. Caldwell, their grief consuming their waking hours. Sadly, the color of mourning would be the most common fashion for the upcoming season.

Jethro left with Percy and Blake Goodman early in September. A local undertaker near Warm Springs, Virginia, had agreed to have the hastily interred remains of Pvt. Will Caldwell shipped by train to Knoxville, Tennessee. Goodman would then transport the body home to Columbia by wagon. Within two weeks, the somber detail would be over. The morning of October 1, 1861, would be a sad day in the town of Columbia. One of its gallant soldiers was returning, never again to hear the call of reveille on this side of Heaven.

Willow began the day giving her servants orders for the funeral dinner. The funeral would be held at the Caldwell home later that morning, but friends would be calling several hours prior, for which Willow would assume the duty of receiving the guests. The stately home of Dr. and Mrs. Adolphus Caldwell was draped in black, the dark ribbons tied around the stone pillars which framed the front door. The body of young Will, too advanced in decomposition to be viewed, had been placed in a solid black lead coffin, draped with the colors of his beloved regiment and Confederacy.

Willow remembered her own son, the same age as Will, off in a faraway place suffering the effects of illness. Kate had composed herself to clasp the hands of the mourners who filed into the home and passed the closed coffin. Beside the funeral bier, ferns and chrysanthemums had been placed to mask the odor emanating from the coffin. A photograph, taken only a few months prior, sat on the small table nearby.

Kate Caldwell was unable to leave the house when the funeral cortege left for Rose Hill Cemetery, east of town. Cordelia remained with Kate, while Willow accompanied Dr. Caldwell with his son's remains. The servants began bringing the funeral meal into the home, as was customary. Funeral biscuits had been prepared, each with a small paper wrapper announcing the passing and funeral of Private William Caldwell. An assortment of funeral cakes and pies were placed on the large Duncan Phyfe table in the formal dining room. Esther, Martha, and Louise, assisted by Lewis, and the servants of Mrs. Caldwell, Fannie and Georgianne, would wait for Willow to commence serving all the mourners a meal consisting of black-eyed peas, ham, cornbread, and greens. An assortment of relishes and eggs were also placed upon the table. Following the burial, a host of friends and family came to support the grieving parents of Private William Caldwell, of the 1st Tennessee.

That evening, Willow and Cordelia could hear the servants downstairs softly singing the spirituals they had come to know. *Steal away, steal away, steal away to Jesus...*As Cordelia slipped away into a night of restless sleep, she hummed the haunting melody.

The 1st Tennessee had begun construction of winter quarters east of Huntersville, Virginia. Many of the regiment, still sick with a variety of infirmities, were given orders for discharge, and furloughs were given to the most ill. The first word of the furlough for Simon Ashby came late in the month of November, 1861. Simon, along with several from Companies A, D and H, were placed on railcars and sent back to Tennessee to recuperate. Some would remain unfit for duty, while others would rejoin their ranks after the winter encampments were on the move.

Willow received word that Simon had contracted pneumonia, brought on by a case of measles. He lingered for several weeks, now too weak to remain in fighting condition. She would travel to Nashville, where the train would arrive sometime in mid-November. Willow's slumberous nightly encounters with her dead sister caused her to consider bringing to light the buried secrets she had been keeping.

Orders were given to get Master Simon's room moved to the lightest and best ventilated room in the upstairs. Cordelia would take up residence in one of the smaller bedrooms for the comfort of her cousin, Simon. Dr. Caldwell was solicited to accompany Willow to Nashville, where an examination could be performed concerning the safety of Simon's further transportation to Columbia. The Nashville Female Academy had been transformed into a hospital, and the residents had been sent home earlier in the fall. Several of the academies in and around the Nashville area had sent their students back home in fear of the Yankees being near the Cumberland River.

Willow, Jethro, and Dr. Caldwell boarded the train from Columbia to Nashville on the morning of November 20. A telegram was sent to Willow announcing that she could find Simon in one of the hospitals located in town. The once thriving Female Academy that was home to Cordelia for many years was now a home for disabled and injured soldiers. The Military Academy where both Simon and Gibson Hughes had been cadets was now Hospital Number 2. Cordelia would remain to supervise the servants and continue her work with the Ladies Aid Society.

While she awaited the return of her aunt and cousin, Cordelia decided to investigate the crates in the carriage house.

The town appeared much different from when Willow and Cordelia had visited the Nashville Hotel earlier that fall. A greater military presence greeted them when they disembarked from the railcar.

"Dr. Caldwell, where should we begin our search?" Willow inquired, feeling a sense of sadness overtake her.

Dr. Caldwell instructed Jethro to find a carriage to take them to the Military Academy first, since it was closest.

"Mrs. Ashby, I want you to put this hanky over your nose when we enter, I don't know what we are in store for," Dr. Caldwell suggested, adjusting the collar of his coat to protect his face from the wind.

Neither Willow nor Dr. Caldwell was prepared for the number of men being taken care of. Beds from the cadet quarters, as well as donated beds from in and around the town, had been brought into large open areas to create makeshift wards. Willow searched for Simon among the men, some delirious with fever, others with amputated limbs wrapped in stiffened bloody bandages. A young woman dressed in a simple work dress and apron approached the pair, her kind smile a welcome site.

"May I help you?" the young lady inquired.

"My name is Dr. Adolphus Caldwell, and this is Mrs. Elijah Ashby. We've come to find her son, Private Simon Ashby. We were told he might be in this hospital."

The nurse searched the room for the hospital matron, locating her near the bed of a wounded soldier.

"Please wait a moment, and I'll ask Mrs. Dunbar if there is anyone here with that name."

She made her way across the rows of soldiers, inquiring of Simon Ashby to the matron. After a few moments, the young nurse returned.

"I'm sorry, there doesn't appear to be anyone here by that name. Have you tried Hospital Number 1? The Female Academy received several soldiers this week from Virginia, I heard. You might try over there. I'm sorry."

Dr. Caldwell and Willow thanked the young lady, then made their way back out onto the street. Jethro was waiting with the carriage driver, and helped Willow into the carriage, her skirts getting caught momentarily on the latch to the carriage door. The driver took them across the street and down another until they were in front of the Nashville Female Academy. The young ladies were now absent from their studies, and soldiers were given accommodation for rest and medical care. Upon entering the large building, Willow recognized Mrs. Sturgeon, who now was doing her part to bring the wounded and sick into the once thriving academy.

"Mrs. Sturgeon. I don't know if you remember me, but I'm Mrs. Elijah Ashby."

"Yes, of course, Mrs. Ashby. How is Miss Cordelia?" she inquired, a smile overtaking her serious countenance.

Thankful for a familiar face, Willow continued, "She is well, thank you. But I'm afraid my son, Simon, has been sent home on furlough. We thought he might be here," she said, hopefully.

Mrs. Sturgeon went to her desk where a list of names had been registered. Searching through her list, she looked up and said, "I'm sorry, Mrs. Ashby. There haven't been any soldiers by that name brought in this week."

Willow was crestfallen. What if something had happened to Simon, and he was no longer alive? Seeing her anguish, Dr. Caldwell spoke up. "Is there perhaps another hospital in town where he could have been sent?"

Mrs. Sturgeon named a series of locations where Simon could have been taken upon arrival to the city. It was decided the pair would make their way to each of the high schools in the city, then find a suitable place to have their lunch before resuming the search.

Willow felt the chill as she entered the first makeshift hospital. How miserable for the soldiers, being sick and cold. No sooner had she made her way into what was once a large hall for study, she saw the pale, brown-haired boy that she recognized as her own. Without a word to Dr. Caldwell, she bolted without care for propriety to her son, who had been sleeping on the large four poster bed that was now a hospital bed.

"Simon! Oh, Simon, I thought we'd never find you!" Willow sobbed, happy to have found her son.

He raised his head weakly from the pillow, dark circles framing eyes that were now flowing with tears. Dr. Caldwell gave the mother and son a moment to embrace, then began his assessment of the boy's condition. As the examination was taking place, a young man with a medical bag approached the pair.

"I'm Dr. Bohannon. Is this your boy?" he inquired, somewhat glad to see another apparent physician in the place.

Willow made their introductions, followed by a moment to discuss her son's condition. As the two doctors conversed, it was decided that perhaps he could be moved, and would make a better recovery if he were home surrounded by his loving family. Dr. Caldwell agreed that they could provide a better environment for recuperation. Arrangements were made, and a litter carrying Simon Ashby was taken to the train station, where Jethro, Willow, and Dr. Caldwell stayed by his side until their arrival in Columbia later that day.

During the days Willow was away, Cordelia was given charge over the servants. She found that she most enjoyed spending time in the kitchen with Esther and Martha. Cordelia continued to prod Martha for details of life at her grandfather's plantation, Dryer Hall. Dr. James Dryer had been widowed after his wife, Abigail, was taken with cholera in 1825. He was left to raise four children: Willow, the oldest, James Jr., Lucretia, and Emma. The youngest of the children, Emma, would also die from the dreaded disease that claimed so many that summer. Dr. Dryer let the capable Dolly, mother of Pharaoh, take over the rearing of the youngest children, while Willow did her best to help her father with the household duties.

"Were you familiar with my mammy, Mammy Cilla?" Cordelia prodded.

Martha seemed to take on a jealous tone to her voice. Not wanting to overstep, she guarded her words carefully.

"Yas'm, I knowd Priscilla. She was just a youngin' when Miz Willow married Massa Ashby. Her mammy was Celine. She worked in the Massa's house. Priscilla was one of Dr. Dryer's favored."

Cordelia heard the way Martha said 'favored,' and wondered why. She and Martha were interrupted by the bell ringing at the front door. Martha quickly excused herself and went into the house to answer the door.

The four crates that Cordelia brought back from Nashville were placed against the back wall of the carriage house. Cyrus was leaning against the straw that was stacked outside the horse stalls. He was smoking a pipe, the rings circling above his head.

"Cyrus, you know better than to be smoking that out here. You want to burn the whole carriage house and stable down?" Cordelia snapped.

Cyrus jumped, not aware Cordelia had walked in.

"Sorry, Miz Cordie."

Cyrus stamped the ember from the pipe on the stone below his feet. Cordelia smiled, then continued, "Now, I have a job for you. Fetch the crow bar and let's start opening those crates."

Cyrus did as instructed, and in short order had the four crates opened for inspection. Cordelia didn't spend too long on the contents of the first crate. It appeared these were the volumes of law books that had lined the walls in her father's study. She made a mental note to make sure these went to Gibson Hughes upon his return. The next two crates contained ledger after ledger from the plantation, mostly in her father's hand. There were some notations that appeared to be from a different hand. She assumed it to be her mother's. There was nothing that seemed too interesting in this crate, so she proceeded to the fourth. When she saw that there were seven individual boxes, each nailed tightly to keep the contents inside, her curiosity got the better of her.

In the first box were dresses, the style of them appearing to be from an earlier time. She found there to be almost ten dresses of different styles. The next box contained slippers, some satin, others leather. The foot of the owner was quite petite. In the next box were personal toiletry items: brush, comb, mirror, toothbrush, and bottles of perfume. Cordelia began to understand. These were items that belonged to her mother. Her father must have had the servants remove all of her belongings after he returned and found her and the baby dead and buried.

The remaining boxes contained articles of men's clothing. Various personal items were also packed inside. As Cordelia continued her search inside the box, she came across a ledger book, similar to the ones of her father. Across the front in dark ink was the name Benton Hallert. Cordelia dropped the ledger as if it were hot coals.

"Wha's de matter, Miz Cordie?" Cyrus asked, noticing the look of horror on Cordelia's face.

Without examining the remaining box, she barked out the order, "Take the hammer and nail these crates shut. I have to get back in the house."

Cordelia hurried out of the carriage house, and Cyrus shook his head, doing as he was told.

Gibson Hughes spent the better part of this gray November day trying to keep the cold rain from dripping on his face. His tent had been leaking since late the previous night. Due to an overwhelming number of furloughs and discharged soldiers, the 1st Tennessee had seen several of its officers out of commission for duty. Gibson was up for picket duty, a task he had grown to hate. The temperature had dropped considerably, and now his fingers began to feel numb as he stood guarding the encampment. He wasn't sure how his friend, Simon, had fared once he was furloughed earlier in the month. Mail hadn't been delivered for three weeks, and Cordelia had been on his mind for the better part of the night. If he lived to see the end of the war, he wanted to make enough money to buy a house and ask her to marry him.

The first days of Simon Ashby's return home were spent sleeping in his own bed, surrounded by his mother and Martha. Dr. Caldwell had made daily visits, bringing what medicine he could to help Simon fight the effects of pneumonia. After his latest examination, he stepped outside the door to speak with Willow.

"I've done all that I can do, Mrs. Ashby. It is now in God's hands. He's young, and that is in his favor. But now we will have to wait and see."

This was news Willow had prayed she wouldn't hear. If he was not to survive, she must do what she always hoped she wouldn't be forced to do.

"Thank you, Dr. Caldwell. We will continue praying and I will do what is necessary to make him comfortable."

Willow led Dr. Caldwell down the stairs to the hallway below. Lewis was waiting at the bottom of the landing to hand the doctor his hat and coat.

After Willow gave the doctor her thanks again, she asked him to tell his wife that she would come to call on her later in the week. Her period of mourning dictated she spend her time of grief at home.

Willow instructed Lewis to go out to the wood pile and stoke the fires in the fireplaces downstairs, then have Jethro and Cyrus fetch logs for the upstairs as well. She then said a prayer for what she was about to do, and climbed the stairs.

Cordelia was sitting at her writing table, penning a letter to Gibson. Willow knocked softly, not walking into the room. Seeing her aunt at the doorway, Cordelia smiled, waiting for her aunt to come in.

"Cordelia, could you please come with me into Simon's room. I must talk to you both."

Setting the pen back in the inkwell, she took hold of her aunt's soft hand and followed her into the sickroom. Simon had been elevated on pillows to help with his breathing, and Martha sat nearby. When he saw his mother and Cordelia enter the room, he offered a weak smile.

"Simon, dear, if you are feeling up to it, I would like to talk with you and Cordelia," Willow said, sitting on the bed beside her son.

Cordelia pulled a chair from the dressing table over to be near her cousin and aunt. Martha sat quietly on the other side of the bed, waiting for her mistress to dismiss her. She never did.

"Simon, Cordelia, there is something I must tell you. I had hoped this day would never come, but I have been visited in my dreams by my dear sister, and I feel I must do what is right."

Martha wanted to stop her mistress from saying another word, but perhaps what the slaves had said about haunts was true. She sat in silence as Willow continued. Simon and Cordelia seemed confused on where the conversation was heading.

"I don't understand, Mother."

Cordelia wondered if she somehow knew about the personal items she found in the crates outside. Willow continued, "I went to Gallatin when your mother was a month from her delivery. She was afraid of your father, and he knew that she had been unfaithful with the young overseer. After she delivered the baby, she began to show signs of childbed fever."

Cordelia had heard this before. *Why did Willow feel she must share this about her mother with Simon?* It was obvious Simon was trying to understand as well.

"Aunt Willow, I know about Mother and my brother dying," Cordelia said.

Willow nervously tugged at the quilt that covered Simon, and forged on with what needed to be done.

"Please, Cordelia. Let me finish."

Cordelia saw Martha's expression take on a look of fear, and she moved in closer to Simon, as if to protect him.

"As I said, your mother knew she didn't have long. Priscilla brought you to her, so that she could tell you goodbye, Cordelia. She then asked for the baby, a boy, to be brought to her so that she could see him one last time."

Willow took her son's hand, and looked at Cordelia as she continued.

"That baby, Simon, was you. I'm so sorry I have misled you all these years, dear."

Cordelia felt as if she had been punched in the stomach. How could everyone have lied so easily to her? Simon's tears began to pool in his eyes, then a large dollop hit his chest, causing him to cough. Willow and Martha both reached out to him, but he waved them away.

"Simon, I did as your mother asked. She was afraid of what Absalom would do, angry as he was. Priscilla, Lucretia, and I vowed he would never know. Your father, Benton Hallert, wanted to take you away, but we agreed that you would come with me. I would petition to take you as well, Cordelia."

Willow's words didn't seem to be registering with Simon, who had just learned the woman he loved as his own beloved Mother was his aunt! Willow paused, then continued.

"During the night, my dear sister passed away. It was then that we devised the lie we told and swore never to share. Your mother was placed in a coffin that Pharaoh and Old Thomas made, and she was laid to rest the following morning. Mammy Cilla hid the baby in her cabin, lying him next to Benny, who was only a month old at the time."

"Why did Mammy Cilla lie to me?" Cordelia sobbed.

"Cordelia, had she told you and you told your Father, he might have come for Simon."

"Mother, why didn't you tell me? I deserved to know Cordelia was my sister," Simon questioned.

Willow now saw that she had caused both Simon and Cordelia heartache by sharing her secret.

"Is that why Mammy Cilla left the paper with your name on it so I would find it?" Cordelia asked, now putting the pieces together.

"Yes, that is why, I'm sure. But I was going to send for you. I tried. Your father..." Willow paused, saying more than she wanted.

"What about Father? Why didn't you come for me if he was so cruel?"

Willow didn't want to go on. She knew the pain that Cordelia was already feeling.

"Why didn't you send for me? You already had my brother. Did you not love me enough?" Cordelia said, choking out the words.

Finally, Martha spoke.

"Miz Willow, I's goin' to tell the chile myself if you don't."

Cordelia wiped her eyes, looking at her aunt in a beseeching manner.

"Cordelia, I sent a letter, begging your father to let you come with me. But he returned my letter, saying that you had died. I thought I had lost you too. I didn't know you were alive until you showed up at my door last spring."

Cordelia buried her head into her hands, trying to stop the sobs that wracked her body. Everything she believed had been a lie. Simon had composed himself, and reached out his hand to his mother.

"I forgive you, Mother. Where is Benton Hallert?" Simon inquired.

Cordelia looked up, without emotion, and said, "My father killed him."

Martha gasped, covering her mouth. Willow wiped the tears that were now flowing from her eyes. Why had she opened this kettle of fish?

"Cordelia, Simon, I am so sorry I have upset you both. With Simon so ill, I thought it should be known to you both. It will never leave this room. You are still my son, Simon, and I love you like my own. Cordelia, it is what your mother wanted."

Cordelia stood and looked at her brother, who was too weak to sit up any longer.

"Simon, I always felt there was something similar to our looks, and now it is apparent why. You were the brother I prayed for, and thought was buried without a name next to my mother."

She leaned down to embrace Simon, and he offered his embrace, weak as it was.

"Cordie, it might take me awhile to understand it all, but I'm glad you found us."

Seeing the exhaustion on his face, Willow stood, taking Cordelia by the hand.

"Simon, I'll return after I have dressed for bed. I will answer any questions you or Cordelia might have. You are both gifts that God has entrusted to me, and I know your mother is watching over you both."

Martha stayed with Simon as Willow and Cordelia went to dress for bed. As she sat with Simon, she thought about the secrets that the Dryer family had carried to their graves. There was yet another secret that would come to light.

Simon's condition slowly improved during the next week, and soon he was able to join the family downstairs for longer periods of time during the day.

Cordelia asked that the conversation between the three of them remain buried, as was her mother. For Simon, the revelation was not as easy to dismiss. Learning about his parentage had caused the boy to develop a melancholy that no one but Cordelia could truly understand.

The matter, for now, was laid to rest. Christmas was less than a week away, and Willow instructed the servants to make the house as festive as possible. The formal parlor was adorned with a Christmas tree and greenery hung from all the entryways in the large house. Willow sat at the harp in front of the large window and played *Silent Night*. Hearing the melody, Cordelia began singing. The impromptu performance brought Simon into the parlor, showing his recuperation was nearly complete. After the song was finished, Simon broke the spell of the moment with an announcement.

"Mother, I guess I should be gettin' back with the boys after Christmas. I reckon the Company will be on the move soon."

Willow didn't want to spoil the holiday with talk of Simon leaving. It had been good to have him home, gaining strength each day, and Dr. Caldwell had cut his daily visits down to once a week. Cordelia walked over to the settee and sat beside him.

"I received a letter yesterday from Gibson, Simon. He asked about you. He said they were suffering terribly from the cold. I am knitting him wool socks and a pair of gloves to send this week," Cordelia said, trying to change the subject.

"Do you think he will get a furlough for Christmas?" Simon asked.

"With so many gone in the regiment, he said not to expect him. I was so hopeful that we would get to spend the holiday together."

News came later in the week from Anna Mosby. Her brothers would not be allowed to return on furlough, nor would her father. Anna had not received word regarding her beau, Sam Walker. The two had become quite serious before he mustered out, and an engagement was expected as soon as the war was over.

Christmas with the war going on cast a shadow on an otherwise happy time for Willow. Cordelia enjoyed spending time with Simon, and the two often spent hours in the warm sunny parlor, talking about their childhoods.

In early January, Simon made his way back to Nashville, and from there he would be sent back to Virginia to join up with the 1st Tennessee, near Romney, Virginia. The servants stood like statues as Simon came down the stairs wearing his frock coat and new woolen breeches. Cordelia had knitted a new scarf and mittens for him, and Willow had given him a small golden cross on a chain.

"Simon, this belonged to my mother. It has protected me all my days since she placed it in my hand on her deathbed. I want you to take it with you to protect and guard you."

Simon bent over to kiss his mother on her cheek, then embraced her. He put the chain over his head, the small cross resting against his chest.

"Thank you, Mother. I will see that it comes back when I return."

Martha hugged Simon, standing on her tiptoes to whisper in his ear, "You come back to us, Massa' Simon."

"You don't have anything to worry about, Martha. I'm fit as a fiddle now!"

Cordelia stepped forward, embracing Simon, almost too tightly.

"Watch out for yourself, or you'll have to answer to your big sister," Cordelia whispered into his ear.

"I will, and please look out for Mother. Thank you, Cordie."

Jethro took Simon's bedroll and haversack out to the carriage. Willow gave him one last embrace, trying not to weep as he walked down the path to the waiting carriage. She watched the carriage round the corner, taking him once again into harm's way.

Chapter 29

Simon arrived in Romney, Virginia, on the 18th of January, 1862. It was here that he and Gibson caught their first sight of the famous General Jackson. The regiment would soon be moving yet again, this time back to their home, Tennessee. Word arrived of the invasion of Tennessee and the fall of Fort Henry. Newspapers in the area reported the invasion into the state by General Ulysses S. Grant of the Union. The battle would usher in the fall of Fort Donelson as well, putting the Cumberland River under Federal control. Some of the Confederate soldiers escaped from Fort Donelson into Nashville, warning the citizens to flee the city. On February 25, the Federal Army, under the command of General Don Carlos Buell, entered Nashville and captured the city. It was then that the Confederate forces abandoned Middle Tennessee.

Newspapers reported the governor, legislators, and other state officials fled to Memphis. The hospitals in the city were quickly occupied by Union forces. The citizens of Middle Tennessee read the accounts of Yankee soldiers taking food and forcing the removal of Confederate flags and banners.

Anna Mosby wrote of the panic that overtook her own town. She told of the steamboat dock being destroyed, as well as bridges across the Cumberland River into the town of Edgefield. What machinery could be transported was taken to the southern Tennessee town of Chattanooga. She reported city officials in Nashville being arrested for treason because they refused to take the oath to support the Union. Cordelia shared the letter with her aunt.

"Aunt Willow, it is all so frightening. Yankees in Nashville arresting law abiding citizens! What if they come here? What shall we do?"

Willow had been hearing the stories from the women at the sewing circle each week. The slaves were talking about freedom coming with the Yankees. One such slave, Cyrus, had been planning for his escape. Every Wednesday, when he went to get the items on Willow's supply list from the dry goods store, he met with the slaves out in the back. They were planning to run away to Nashville, offering their help to the Yankee army. It wouldn't be necessary; the Yankees were coming to Columbia.

Willow instructed Lewis to gather the silver and place it in sacks. Esther was given directions for carefully packing Elijah's sword and saddle in the empty trunk upstairs that Cordelia had brought home from Nashville. Jethro was told to dig a hole in the carriage house where all the items would be buried. If the Yankees made it as far as Columbia, which she doubted, there would be time to take their most prized possessions to the carriage house, where they could be quickly put in the hole and covered with hay from the horse stable. If the Yankees came, they would be ready. Cordelia wished there was a man in the house to protect them.

In March, the Federal Army made their way into Columbia, Tennessee. Cordelia and Willow had paid a call on Mrs. Kate Caldwell. Since burying her young son, Will, Mrs. Caldwell hadn't left the house except to attend Sunday church services. The afternoon had warmed up considerably, and Willow suggested Jethro could drive the team back to the stable. It was good to be able to walk and enjoy the early spring flowers that were just starting to poke their heads above the grass. Cordelia, linking arms with her aunt, felt no matter what revelation Willow had shared regarding her mother, she had forgiven the lies that needed to be told. As the two continued their pleasant walk, they could hear someone yelling near the end of their street. Willow turned, seeing a young boy dressed as a soldier running up the street.

"Yankees a'coming!!! They's coming into town, Ma'am!" the boy said.

He quickly passed by them, not waiting to hear any questions. Willow's face drained of color, and she felt her knees go weak.

"There's no time to warn anyone, Cordelia. We must hurry home."

The two women made their way down the street and up the walk to the front door. Willow let Cordelia enter first, then quickly turned the key to lock the door.

"Martha! Lewis! Come here, quickly!" Willow yelled.

Cordelia had never heard her aunt so much as raise her voice. Hearing her yell for the servants caused them to come into the parlor, winded from the sprint to reach their mistress.

"What's da matter, Miz Ashby?" Lewis blurted, trying to catch his breath.

"Lewis, George Hanson's boy just saw Yankees coming into town. They're here," Willow said, sounding calmer than seconds before.

By the time she finished her sentence, Louise, Esther, and Jethro had made their way into the parlor as well, each with a look of terror on their faces.

"Whats we gonna do, Miz Willow?" Louise asked, frightened.

"Where is Cyrus?" Willow asked.

Martha spoke first, "He go to town, Miz Willow. He been hangin' 'round with no counts behind de dry goods store. He be waiting for de Yankees."

Cordelia looked at her aunt, who remained unruffled by the announcement.

"I'm sure the Yankees will make him work harder than he ever did here," Willow pronounced.

Willow put the news about Cyrus being in town without her permission out of her mind and continued, "The Yankees have arrived in Columbia, and we have to be brave. I don't think they will harm an old woman and her servants. We pose them no threat."

After evening prayers were said, the servants were dismissed to their quarters. Cordelia and Willow, behind the closed pocket doors of the parlor, discussed Cyrus' plotting to run away.

"Aunt Willow, what do you think will become of Cyrus?" Cordelia asked.

"I don't know, dear. I can only hope the others will remain with us, as I have always been fair and just with them."

The Federal occupation of Columbia left many women in the town afraid to go out of their homes. Willow Ashby, having no male relatives living in the house, kept a loaded pistol inside the drawer of the library table in the entry hall. She had resigned herself to use it, should anyone try to molest or injure a member of her household. One evening, late in the month of October, a knock came during their evening prayers. Martha looked at her mistress, her dark eyes wide with fright. Willow put her finger up to her mouth, instructing all in the room to be quiet.

"Martha, you may answer the door," Willow instructed.

Cordelia moved closer to her aunt, grabbing her hand tightly. In the entry hall, Martha opened the door, seeing two Union soldiers standing on the other side.

"Where's your master?" the young soldier snapped.

Martha didn't much like the Yankee soldiers, seeing how they took whatever they wanted from the town's people, and now they had decided to start with Willow Ashby.

"Miz Ashby is having evening prayers," Martha replied, never looking the soldier in the eye.

Willow came into the hallway, seeing the two soldiers nearly inside her doorway.

"I am Mrs. Ashby. What is the reason for your interruption of our evening prayers?" she said, her voice remaining calm.

The young soldier was taken aback, as if his own mother had just reprimanded his rude behavior.

"Beg your pardon, Ma'am, but we are just checking for Johnny Rebs who were seen near the Duck River headed this way. You won't mind us having a look, will you?"

Martha stepped in front of the two soldiers, stopping their entrance.

"You wipe yor muddy boots befo' you comes in this house!" Martha snapped.

"You may search if you like, but there are no soldiers hiding in this house," Willow said without emotion.

The two soldiers pushed past Martha, looking first in the formal parlor, then into the parlor across the hall. It was then that they saw Cordelia and the other servants, remaining motionless. The soldiers were about the same age as Cordelia, and the soldier who had yet to speak tipped his kepi hat when he saw her. She remained calm, not showing her fear. The soldiers went throughout the house, not bothering to take anything. They had been instructed by their commanding officer not to bother anything, only to search for rebels. Willow waited at the foot of the stairs as the doors upstairs were opened, but nothing taken. When they went to the third floor, the soldier called down to send a light up to search the attic. Jethro was sent with a lantern, where the two soldiers searched the entire third floor. When they were satisfied no one was hiding in the house, they came back to the parlor.

"We will be going, Mrs. Ashby. If you see any of the Rebs, you best not let them in. You will be arrested, Ma'am."

Willow thanked them for making their search quick, and showed them back to the door. When they had left, she waited until she saw the torch lights going to the next house. She spoke in a whisper, "We must be careful. They will be watching the house."

Word came from both Simon and Gibson describing their transport back to Tennessee. Upon arriving in Knoxville, there was not adequate transportation, and it was there the two were separated. The Right Wing, Companies A-E, of which Gibson was a part, were sent to Bridgeport and Chattanooga. There, they would guard important bridges over the Tennessee River. The Left Wing, Companies F-K, which Simon had rejoined, was sent on to Corinth, Mississippi. The letters were short, but each told of their movement and that they were well.

It was the letter that came from Anna Mosby that Yankees were marching down the Franklin-Nashville Pike, dangerously close to her home, that scared them. Her mother, Bess, and Anna hastily hid their belongings in a vacant bedroom upstairs, locking the door. Anna would later laugh at their naiveté. Two of their fieldhands escaped with the marching army. Anna never saw them again.

Simon would fight in his first battle, arriving at Shiloh on the second day of the battle, April 6, 1862. He saw Anna Mosby's brothers, Joel and Jed, waiting for the order to charge. In a moment, the handsome favorite son of Jennie Mosby would receive his death wound. In the blink of an eye, a Yankee minié ball would tear through his chest, the life leaving his body before he struck the ground. Simon heard the whiz of the shot that struck the soldier next to him, a splattering of skull and blood spraying his face. He fell back, thinking he himself had been hit. A young lieutenant grabbed his arm, pulling him forward. It was then that Simon found his courage. Hearing the order to charge with bayonets fixed, he found the meanness that was required and, with all the rage he could muster, let out a scream that would raise the hair on the Yankees' heads when they heard it. In the melee that ensued, Simon would see the famous general, Albert Sidney Johnston, lying on the ground, killed during the battle.

Stepping over dead and dying Union soldiers, Simon forged onward. Over the noise and smoke, he heard the words that the Yankees were retreating.

Simon took part in rummaging through the Yankees' camp, a treasure trove like he hadn't seen in months. Money, new pants, shirts, and extra rations lay strewn about the camp. In the Yankees' haste to retreat, the spoils of war lay about the camp as if a banquet had been prepared for the Confederates.

Gibson and the Right Wing would arrive April 7, too late to take part in the fighting. Following the bloody Battle of Shiloh, the 1st Tennessee took stock of their losses. The Left Wing was hit hard, losing large numbers at the battle. After two days of fighting, almost 24,000 Confederate and Union soldiers had been captured, wounded, killed or were missing.

Gibson and Simon made their way to Corinth, Mississippi, where the regiment went under reorganization. The command of the Army of Tennessee had been given to General Beauregard after the death of General Johnston. However, Beauregard had resigned. The command was then given to General Braxton Bragg. Both wings would reunite in Corinth, Mississippi, where Simon would find Gibson and tell him of seeing Anna Mosby's brothers during the battle. He tried as best he could to recount the final moments of Joel Mosby. Simon and Gibson would each report the news back home, as well as give accounts of waiting in Mississippi for marching orders.

Chapter 30

The battle report reached home within a day of the battle, thanks to the telegraph. Newspapers began telling of the carnage at Shiloh. It would be days before the staggering number of lives lost would be made public.

Willow sent Cyrus to fetch a paper from town, praying that Simon's name would not be listed as a casualty. Cordelia waited on the front porch of her aunt's home, watching as people made their way into town to get information about the battle.

As she waited, her thoughts kept straying to the conversation she had been part of just a month before. No wonder Mammy Cilla never gave her a satisfying answer when she asked about her baby brother. How could her father be such a monster? She could hardly blame her Aunt Willow for not coming back to take her, knowing that her father had told her she had died! *That is some fine stock I come from. A lying, murdering, heartless father, and a mother who was unfaithful.*

Cordelia saw Cyrus slowly plodding up the street, carrying a ripped copy of the newspaper under his arm. He carried a crumpled copy of the casualty list as if it were one of her uncle's prized swords. Unable to read, Cyrus didn't even realize the paper was upside down in his hand.

Cordelia jumped up and walked quickly down the steps to meet Cyrus.

"Hurry, Cyrus! You're as slow as dripping molasses!"

"Yas'm, Miz Cordie. I's hurrin'," Cyrus replied.

He handed both papers to her, waiting for her to make a comment about the battle. She took the papers and disappeared into the house, leaving Cyrus standing on the porch. He walked to the back of the house where he would join Jethro in the garden.

"Aunt Willow, the papers have arrived," Cordelia announced.

Willow put her needlepoint on the settee beside her, and Cordelia scanned the names of those who were on the dreaded list. Cordelia noticed the names of two local young men, and Willow commented they must pay a call on both families later. Once again, Simon and Gibson were spared.

The following week, an envelope trimmed in black was brought in with the rest of the mail. Cyrus came through the back door, handing the mail to Martha.

"I's leavin' soon, Martha," he said, trying to keep his voice to a whisper.

Martha looked over her shoulder, then said with a haughty tone,

"You sho' you not bitin' off mo' than you can chew, boy?"

Cyrus turned on the bravado, something which didn't impress Martha.

"I'm sho' the Yankee boys will put you in the army to try and kill Massa Simon. Is dat' what you want?" Martha questioned.

Cyrus felt a pang of guilt over his decision to join up with the Yankees, but only for a moment.

"I don' has nothin' agin' Massa Simon, only dat' he jes' another massa."

Martha heard the sound of Cordelia's shoes coming down the stairway, and motioned for Cyrus to get back to his chores.

"Miz Cordie, da' mail come. Looks like bad news."

Cordelia took the envelope with black border and turned it over to reveal the sender.

"Oh no! It's from Mrs. Mosby," Cordelia announced with a lump rising in her throat.

Martha liked the Mosbys. They were kind to her, and she remembered the young man who had stayed with Willow last year as polite and handsome.

"It says Joel was killed at Shiloh. She doesn't know where he was taken to be buried. Poor Mrs. Mosby. She loved him so."

Cordelia went to her room to send a letter of condolence to the Mosby family. With the Union Army in and around Nashville, travel to Franklin would be out of the question for now. Willow advised against Cordelia making any trips away from Columbia. The trains were full of people either getting away from Nashville or soldiers riding the rails.

Willow also sent her condolences to Jennie Mosby and her daughter, Anna. The two women had made a friendship when she accompanied her daughter to Columbia earlier in the summer. She was sure the loss would be almost more than Jennie could bear. No mention was made of Jed or Evan Mosby, so it was assumed neither was wounded during the battle.

Letters arrived the beginning of August for Willow and Cordelia. Simon told his mother of the awful battle at Shiloh, and how he saw the young Mosby fall to his death. He shared that the regiment had retreated to Tupelo, Mississippi, where their lack of activity had given way to boredom. To pass the time, he had taken to playing a game called 'chuck-a-luck', a game with dice. It was quite popular among the men, and he had started becoming successful in earning extra money from his pards, Dooley Eldridge and Jack Weiss. What he didn't tell his mother was that the men had been using the lice that had overtaken their bodies in races and also for money. There wasn't a soldier in the war who hadn't taken on an army of graybacks onto his own body.

The revelation that her son had taken to gambling was disconcerting, but she thought it best to overlook his confessions and write about other things. Simon complained of the new commander, General Bragg. Most of the young men had seen all they cared to of war, and when their one year enlistment was over, decided to take their pay and go back to their farms. Simon explained that he couldn't leave now; he was committed to whipping the Yankees out of the South.

He shared that the orders were given to move, and within the next day he would be heading north to Chattanooga. He promised to write when they were camped once again. Willow folded the letter, placing it inside the top drawer of her desk. She had saved each letter, and often reread them when she began to worry about her son.

Gibson had been faithful to write to Cordelia, as was she to him. He didn't share the details of the battle he fought in, sparing her more worry. He asked about home, Mrs. Ashby, and Martha. He also asked about the trip to Nashville. She had forgotten to tell him about the crates. She would tell him in her next letter. She decided not to share the secret about Simon's birth. He shared that several members of their regiment had left the army, their year's service over. He was upset about the fact that those men with twenty or more slaves were allowed to go home as well. He wished he could come home to Goodlettsville to see his mother and, of course, for a chance to see the pretty Cordelia Barlow.

Gibson and Simon had boarded railcars in Mobile, Alabama, to Atlanta, Georgia. Finally, the Army of Tennessee stopped off in Chattanooga. Beginning on August 19, 1862, Bragg would march them into Kentucky, taking two months to reach the town of Perryville. Before the army could start the march, Gibson Hughes was ordered to General Bragg's tent, along with several other young soldiers. Making his way through the rows of tents, he spied his friend from the Western Military Institute. Gibson remembered Sam Davis back in Virginia and the fearless look in his eye during the second day's battle at Shiloh.

"Are you going to see General Bragg, Sam?" Gibson asked, noticing several other soldiers coming in behind them.

"Looks like they are too," Sam ventured, looking back over his shoulder at the other young men.

Sam Davis, Gibson Hughes, and the group of soldiers made their way into the tent of their commanding officer. General Bragg had planned a daring project, and Gibson and Sam, along with a select group of Confederates, would be part of it. Following the meeting with General Bragg, Gibson would part company with his brigade, and would become part of a covert operation. He would now become part of Coleman's Scouts. From here on out, he would be operating behind enemy lines, gathering intelligence on the movement of Union troops and other imperative information. Their commander, Captain Shaw, would be given the alias of E. Coleman, and that would be the only name used to identify him within his own scouts or the Confederate leadership.

For the remainder of 1862, the letters from Simon Ashby and Gibson Hughes would cease. The women, whose prayers never ceased to remember them each evening, continued to read the troop movement news in the Columbia paper. In the Battle of Perryville, where Simon and Dooley Eldridge saw their own line cut down around them, they miraculously left the battlefield unscathed. It seemed they had a band of angels encamped around them, protecting them from the cannonball and shot.

Late in 1862, Simon and the 1st Tennessee retreated from Kentucky. The soldiers were starving, not having received rations until their retreat to Camp Dick Robinson. After receiving their three days' worth of rations, they set fire to the storehouses that would have supplied rations to the South for a year.

The army arrived in Knoxville around the 20th of October, 1862. When the soldiers finally reached Murfreesboro, the men from companies A, B, and C, of the Rock City Guards were consolidated into one company. Gibson Hughes was not with his company, having been sent to work with Coleman's Scouts. It was then, while the Union army had moved out of Columbia, that the residents finally breathed a sigh of relief, for a time.

Cordelia had made a rare trip from the house, taking Martha along. The two had walked to the post office, where Cordelia sent a shipment of socks, underwear, and gloves. Not having the exact location of the 1st Tennessee, she hoped the latest address would find Simon and Gibson. She was on her return trip home when she saw a horse tied to the gate in the rear of the house. She pulled Martha closer, fearful that a rogue Yankee soldier was hiding in the stable, bumming for whatever could be taken. She quickly walked into the house, meeting Esther in the front hallway.

"Where is Aunt Willow, Esther?" she blurted.

Esther could see her mistress was shaken, so she quickly replied,

"She done gone to the hospital; she took bread down this mornin', Miz Cordie."

"You get Lewis and Jethro, and stay inside. I think there is someone in the stable."

"Miz Cordie, you cain't go out there," Martha advised.

Cordelia didn't know the first thing about shooting a gun, but she took the loaded pistol in her shaking hand and went out to the stable. The horses inside whinnied as she paused outside, and she almost dropped the loaded weapon. Her legs shook beneath her skirt and layers of petticoats, giving her little support as she tried to move forward. She slowly opened the door, waiting for her eyes to adjust to the dim light within. The two horses of Willow Ashby were clearly nervous, knowing something was amiss.

She must've gasped without realizing it when she saw a shadow move from behind the large gray mare.

"Stop! I have a gun and I'll blow you clean to Richmond!" she said, surprising herself.

"Put the gun down, Cordie! It's me, Gibson!" the familiar voice said in a muted command.

It was then that she saw the face of Gibson Hughes, quite different from when she saw him last. His hair had grown over his collar, and the whiskers on his face were trimmed, giving him an older appearance. His coat appeared to be similar to the Union officers who had been camped around the Athenaeum. Cordelia put the gun on the oat barrel, and walked over to where the soldier stood. Not thinking of proper decorum, she let Gibson pull her close to embrace her. Without care, she hugged him back.

"What are you doing here, Gibson? Is Simon with you?"

Gibson shouldn't have said anything, but felt he might not see her again, and wanted her to know why he had stopped writing to her. He only shared that he was part of a special unit, and that he no longer was in troop movement with Simon. He was on his way to another location, but wanted to see her on his way out of Nashville.

"You've been in Nashville? Can you stay, for tonight?" Cordelia pleaded.

Gibson found he couldn't leave Cordelia, not yet. He hugged her once again, breathing in the lilac perfume that filled his nostrils. He couldn't remember the last time he had smelled something so pleasant.

"Yes, I'll stay tonight. But I have to leave, first light. It isn't safe for me to be here."

"Thank you! Let me bring in your horse. You won't want anyone seeing it tied up outside."

Cordelia took the horse and led the large animal inside the stable, letting Gibson tie him in the back stall. He then picked up the pistol, taking the bullet out of the chamber.

"Do you know how to use this? I think General Bragg would have conscripted you right here!"

The two shared a laugh at the spectacle Cordelia must have displayed. She took the pistol, then said, "Come with me, quickly. The sooner you are in the house, the better."

Gibson pulled his coat up around his neck, put his hat back squarely on his head, and followed Cordelia into the back door of the house.

Willow was surprised to see the tall form of Gibson Hughes standing in the dining room when she returned from the hospital. Cordelia relayed the events of the afternoon, and Willow instructed the servants to make a meal like they had not seen in a long time for the young soldier. Following a meal that practically depleted their storehouse, the lights were kept low so as not to draw attention to their visitor from the street. Gibson didn't engage in conversation about his reason for being apart from the 1st Tennessee, saying only that he would try to come back to see them whenever he could. Willow remained in the parlor that evening with Cordelia and Gibson. Having closed the inner shutters, it was here that they felt safe to visit with him.

The next morning, a sack of biscuits, ham, and apples was brought from the kitchen. Gibson was given a new shirt and long underwear, for which he was most grateful.

"I can't thank you enough, Mrs. Ashby. Please tell no one that you saw me," Gibson instructed.

Willow smiled, taking his hand in hers.

"God go with you, Mr. Hughes. No one will know you were here."

He turned to Cordelia, who was wiping the tears that had suddenly pooled in her eyes. Willow walked to the window, giving the two a moment of privacy.

"It was worth almost being shot to see you again," he said, smiling at the thought of her with the pistol.

"Please be careful, and come home to me, Gibson."

Gibson and Cordelia embraced and, without a care for who might see him, he quickly kissed Cordelia. He tipped his cap, bidding both women goodbye.

Cordelia watched as Gibson quickly made his way in the early light to the stable. Within a few moments, he was out of her sight.

Chapter 32

Cyrus took his knapsack and made his way into the Union camp outside of Nashville. Upon his arrival, he was quickly given his assignment. The army was heading for Murfreesboro, and Cyrus would move with the army. Instead of getting north, Cyrus would be heading south. He had traded the life of a slave for more of the same, but with the Union army.

The temperature had started to fall markedly over Middle Tennessee. The soldiers in the Union Army were given more rations than their Southern counterparts. Cyrus was able to at least have meager rations, for which he was thankful. The group of freed slaves that made up his detail was quickly put to work building Fortress Rosecrans, named after the Union General. The large earthen fort was the largest ever built in North America.

Simon Ashby was thankful for the warm gloves that his mother and Cordelia had sent. He wished he could get warm. It was during one such moment of cursing the cold that word came into the camp that the Yankees were moving towards their line of picket. It was Christmas, and Simon had wished he could be home, sitting with his mother and Cordelia. Before his thoughts could take him from the battle that was about to take place, his regiment was ordered to move forward on the attack. The Yankees began shooting into the lines, but confusion soon set in. Simon could hear soldiers yelling to cease fire, as they were firing into their own line. The color bearer ran past Simon, urging the men behind to follow him. Simon moved, loading and firing as he did.

Simon heard the whizz of the minié ball before he actually felt it strike his arm. The ball struck him just above the elbow, causing him to curse loudly. The wound paralyzed his arm, causing him to drop for a moment to the ground. Passing by him, General Cheatham implored his men to move forward and follow him. Simon tried to pick up his rifle and follow his general, but his arm couldn't take the weight of the rifle. The Confederates were able to push the enemy back, having nearly slaughtered the Federals.

Simon made his way to the rear of the line, stepping over many a dead Bluecoat. The battlefield was nothing short of pure carnage; dead horses, surrounded by the wounded and the dying, could be seen amidst the charge of the Gray. As the Federal army moved some five miles back from their original position, it was safe for the wounded to be removed from the field. Walking towards the line of wounded who could walk back to the field hospital, Simon caught sight of a familiar face lying on the ground. Poor Dooley was worse off than Simon, as the shot had caught him in the lower abdomen. A gut shot was mortal, and Dooley's intestines protruded through his blood-soaked coat.

The poor boy was trying to push the mangled mass back into the gaping wound, a sight that almost caused Simon to wretch. He sat on the ground beside his friend, taking his canteen from his shoulder.

"Simon, you tell my mamma I was brave. It don't hurt none too bad."

Dooley began to convulse, and he lifted his bloody hand to Simon.

"Hold on, Dooley. I'll get you help."

Simon looked around him, and everywhere seemed to be soldiers with arms or legs torn from their bodies. He looked back to Dooley, whose eyes had fixed on something not of this world. The look of terror had all but left his face. Simon didn't even get to say goodbye. He tried to stop the tears, but had to let them flow as he closed the eyes of his friend. Simon stood and made his way back to the line of walking wounded. His arm had begun to throb, and he felt as though his legs were as wobbly as a newborn colt.

When he finally reached the makeshift hospital, the wounded had been placed inside a barn, out of the cold. Simon hadn't even noticed how cold he was; he was already numb. An orderly quickly looked at the wound on Simon's arm. He saw that the ball had struck his haversack first, cutting a gash about four inches long. He would keep his arm, and would be stitched and sent back to his regiment.

The 1st Tennessee moved towards Chattanooga. Simon had been spared serious injury, but he couldn't help but think of poor Dooley lying so pitifully on the battlefield. He didn't even know if he got a proper burial. As he continued to march with what was left of the Maury Grays, he thought about his friend, Gibson Hughes. He knew that Gibson had been taken out of the regiment along with a few other fellows, but news didn't trickle down to Simon.

General Bragg had retreated back to Shelbyville, Tennessee, and it would be here that Simon would spend the rest of the winter, spring and early summer. His wound had healed miraculously, with no signs of infection. He wanted to come home, but had witnessed two soldiers being shot for making a trip home without leave granted. It caused the young soldier to think twice about striking out on his own for a quick visit.

Gibson spent a good portion of the winter riding with two other scouts in and around northern Georgia. While in Georgia, a local plantation owner and his wife had given Gibson and his fellow scouts a warm bed for the night, in exchange for killing three Yankee soldiers who had been bumming for food in the owner's smokehouse. The scouts had come upon them quite by surprise, shooting all three before they could stuff their loot into their haversacks.

A quick letter was written to Cordelia and Gibson's mother before he left the plantation house the following day. The planter's wife promised to take his letters to the post. She fixed the soldiers a small sack of victuals, for which they were thankful. Before the first rays of light, their horses' hooves crunched the frosted ground as they disappeared into the woods.

Chapter 33

The Emancipation Proclamation was issued on January 1, 1863. Slaves all across the South, according to the proclamation by President Lincoln, were to be free, but many did not leave the plantations. Those who decided to leave found themselves between the armies' lines, hoping to be taken in by the Union Army. Willow had read the Proclamation. Since the Yankee army was camped in and around Columbia, the slaves were keeping watchful eyes on freedom.

Cyrus had run off with several of the slaves from the dry goods store, leaving Jethro to be the main gardener and groom. Willow expected that soon the rest of her servants would leave as well. Christmas had been a somber time for Willow and Cordelia. There had been no contact with Gibson, as he left no location to which a letter could be sent. Simon had sent word following the battle at Perryville that he was moving to Murfreesboro, but no letters had arrived since the end of November.

Willow and Cordelia, along with Martha and Louise, began sewing for the soldiers in the 1st Tennessee. Simon's last letter had mentioned how in need the soldiers had become, as their clothing was becoming threadbare.

With the new year came hard times for Southern families under Union occupation. Those who didn't have Union troops camped near their homes were suffering the effects of the Union blockades of Southern ports.

Willow had prepared as best as she could, keeping back meat in the small smokehouse, as well as enlarging the contents of her root cellar during the plentiful harvest earlier in the year. The meals Esther prepared were less elaborate as the third year of the war began. While they were not starving, there were many days that Willow asked Esther to be creative with the ingredients that were coming in short supply. The Federal blockade had made even the coffee that many a Southerner enjoyed impossible to purchase. The soldiers suffered the most, having to partake of rations that were spoiled or having to do without altogether.

News of President Lincoln's Emancipation Proclamation came on the heels of the battle of Stones River. Willow nervously waited for Jethro to return with the battle news and casualty lists from Maury County. Upstairs in her sunny bedroom, Cordelia sat with the bed quilt draped around her shoulders, warding off the chill to which she and the rest of the household had grown accustomed.

Since Cyrus had taken flight with the other Negroes who gathered behind the dry goods store, the task of cutting and collecting wood for the fireplaces in Willow's house had fallen on Jethro. Fires were lit before bedtime and again first thing in the morning, but the rest of the day layers were worn to keep winter's chill at bay. Rather than spending extra money to purchase oil for the lamps, Willow asked the servants to burn pine knots in tin pans. The Northern blockade had reached Columbia, and even the material for dresses that had been readily available at the beginning of the war was now scarce. Women had taken to turning their dresses and knitting their own gloves.

Cordelia sat at her writing desk, holding the quilt around her as she tried to write a letter to Anna Mosby. Her thoughts kept shifting to the crate in the stable, and the articles of clothing that belonged to Benton Hallert. How could her father be a judge, an upholder of the law, and commit such a deed? She was saddened at the thought. She turned to her dressing table, where Pharaoh's whitlin's were displayed. *What has become of you, Pharaoh? Did you and Mammy Cilla get sold together, along with the rest of the family? I'll find you...*

In just a few months, Cordelia would be celebrating her twenty-first birthday. Her father's will bequeathed her a sum of money, to be given on that day. She set her mind to helping Willow with whatever needs she would have to keep food on their table, but also to find and purchase her father's servants. If President Lincoln's proclamation was true, perhaps they were already free. She knew they were sold to someone in

Chattanooga, but that was so far away. A knock on her door startled her, causing her to flinch.

"Cordelia, I'm sorry if I startled you. Jethro brought the paper in this afternoon," Willow said, pausing for a moment. "Simon has been wounded."

Cordelia stood, and the quilt fell to the floor.

"Wounded? How badly is he hurt?" Cordelia asked, feeling a wave of fear overtake her.

Willow took Cordelia's hand in hers, leading her to the small settee at the foot of her bed.

"It lists him as wounded, but nothing more. We must trust in Providence that he is back to health. Surely we would have heard by now. It has been a month since the battle."

Cordelia couldn't help but be concerned for Gibson's welfare. She wasn't sure if he was alive or dead at this point. He had confided in her that he was not with his regiment, but nothing more. She hoped he would come to visit them again, as she had begun to have stronger feelings for him.

"Aunt Willow, when will the war end?" Cordelia asked.

Willow felt a tear trail down her cheek, thinking of her son.

"Cordelia, join me in the parlor. I think our evening prayers should include our asking for strength and courage."

That evening, Willow, Cordelia, and the servants knelt in prayer. Following the nightly ritual, Willow stood, facing the servants who had been with her for many years.

"I'm sure you have heard from other Negroes in town that Mr. Lincoln has made a law freeing the servants living in our country," Willow began.

Jethro, Esther, Martha, and Lewis had been talking of nothing else since talk of Lincoln's Proclamation came down earlier in the year. Cyrus had been right, *Jubilo was comin'*. They waited quietly for Willow to continue.

"While I don't agree with Mr. Lincoln's Proclamation, I can't stop you from leaving. You've each been with this family for many years. I would like for you to remain with me, but if you are planning to leave, please tell me."

Martha was the first to speak. She looked her mistress straight in the eye.

"Miz Willow, I's been with you fo' mo' years than I wuz with my own mammy. I don' reckon I be goin' nowhere. You's all I got."

Cordelia thought of Mammy Cilla and Pharaoh. What would become of them?

"Jethro, will you and Esther be staying on?" Willow asked. Her beseeching gaze caused them both to look down at their feet.

"Miz Willow, we's too old ta' folla' de Yankees. Dis is home ta' us," Jethro replied, his hands nervously twisting his cap.

Willow thanked them, then looked to Louise, who had asked to be bought many years before.

"Louise, how do you feel about staying on with us?" Willow inquired.

"Miz Willow, de Yankee soldiers scare me. I wants to stay with you."

Willow patted Louise's hand, thanking her. Cordelia was comforted in knowing their family would stay together. Willow couldn't offer the servants anything more than a place to live and food to eat, in return for their service. In reality, nothing had changed.

Chapter 39

During the Spring of 1863, a Federal reconnaissance party left Franklin, Tennessee in the direction of Spring Hill. The Union command would find themselves within range of Confederate General Earl Van Dorn and his unsympathetic cavalry near Thompson's Station. Word reached Columbia that a fight had broken out, with the Federals running through their ammunition. When forced to surrender, the Federals gave General Van Dorn his finest moment as an officer.

For the better part of the summer, Federal forces occupied Spring Hill and built a garrison to protect the railroad that ran through the town. Gibson had planned to make a trip back through the area to see Cordelia. Several of the scouts had planned a meeting with Coleman, and it was during this rendezvous that Gibson took his leave to make a chance meeting right under the nose of the Federal Army.

Willow, Cordelia, and the servants had spent the better part of the summer tending to the vegetable garden in the rear of the property. Many of the residents of Columbia tried to grow what food they could, while trying to keep it hidden from the foraging armies moving through the area. Cordelia didn't hear the two soldiers make their silent approach from the alley behind her aunt's home. Looking for food, they noticed the two gray mares inside the small stable.

"Aunt Willow, Yankees!" gasped Cordelia.

She wiped the sweat from her forehead on her apron, yanking the sleeve of her aunt's simple cotton day dress. Willow Ashby stood, brushing back the stray hairs that had fallen out of her braid and into her eyes. Defiantly she walked towards the soldiers.

"Those are my mares. If it is food you need, I will give you food for your haversacks."

The two Federal soldiers, dirty and hungry, had a look of disdain overtake their faces.

"Curtis, I believe this here rebel done give us permission to help ourselves to her garden," the smaller of the two remarked.

Cordelia wished she still had the pistol that she carried sometimes when gathering the eggs from the chicken coop in her apron. The one soldier smiled when he saw Cordelia. His gaze caused her skin to feel like it did when she had crawled through a spider's web with Benny.

"Jethro, fetch some roasting ears for the soldiers," Willow instructed.

The soldier advanced on the group, his gun pointed at them. Cordelia grabbed Willow's hand. Clearly, the soldiers had no intentions of accepting the small basket of roasting ears Jethro picked out of the basket.

"Now you just do as yur told and nobody has to git hurt."

The servants of Willow Ashby were now face to face with the Union soldiers whom so many in town had wanted to come to set them free. Seeing them with a gun pointing at their faces lessened their fascination with the idea.

"Please, we have nothing in the smokehouse. We will give you food," Willow implored.

The other soldier, Curtis, unaware of the guns pointing at them from behind the summer kitchen, advanced toward Cordelia.

"You there, pretty gal. Where you been hiding all the food?" Curtis said, inching closer to Cordelia.

Cordelia recognized the look the soldier had in his eye; it reminded her of the devil Crenshaw who was the overseer at Fairview.

"Take the corn and get off our property, Yankee scum," Cordelia blurted, her anger rising.

The soldier, clearly perturbed by Cordelia's defiance, grabbed Jethro and shoved him towards the smokehouse. The other soldier pointed the gun at Cordelia. Her knees felt as though they would fold beneath her skirt, but before she could collapse from fright, the soldier pushed her towards the stable.

"If you don't show us where the old rebel woman has stashed the food, we'll be eating those two mares in the stable," he sneered.

Willow screamed at the soldier who had accosted her niece. The sound of her voice startled Cordelia.

"Stay away from those mares! There is no buried food. You can take the chickens and the corn, but leave my mares alone."

Jethro and the soldier returned carrying a ham, yams, and turnips from the box hidden in the summer kitchen. The other soldier had pushed Cordelia into the stable. She knew Lewis had brought the silver and other family heirlooms out to the stable, burying them in the stalls. Thankfully the stalls needed cleaning, and the soldiers wouldn't be able to see the disturbed earth.

"Be a good gal and show me where the rest of yur food is hidden," he snapped.

"You found what little food we had. There is no more, I tell you."

The soldier wasn't so sure about that. He saw the crates behind Cordelia and hollered for the other soldier. He brought the servants and Willow at gunpoint into the stable.

"What'd ya find, Curtis?"

"It looks like they's got food afterall. You, boy, come and open this up," he snapped at Jethro.

Willow grabbed Cordelia's arm and pulled her close. The servants stood around their mistress, not saying a word. Jethro took the crowbar and began to pull the nails from the first crate. Cordelia remembered seeing the items in the crate, and hoped she wouldn't have to see them again. After seeing the contents of the first crate, Curtis slammed the lid down. Disappointed there was no food or liquor, he turned to the frightened ensemble. He ordered the other soldier to untie the two gray mares. Willow pleaded, as the mares were like pets to her. He grabbed Jethro's arm.

"Boy, you have been emancipated. We need a good groom for our horses, and seems you won't be needing one anymore, ma'am," he snickered.

The look of horror overtook Willow's face. She asked them once more to leave the mares, but it was no use. At that point, Jethro finally spoke.

"Massa, please lets me brang along my missus. She been cookin' for Miz Willow fo' a long time."

Willow looked at Esther, whose dark eyes were wide with fright. Martha moved in closer to her mistress. Willow touched the sleeve of Esther.

"God go with you, Esther," she whispered, her voice sounding resigned to the situation.

The soldiers nodded their head, then pushed the women and Lewis out of the stable. Jethro took his hat off, his eyes not making contact with Willow's.

"Goodbye, Miz Willow. You's been good to me. Thank you," he blurted.

"Goodbye, Jethro. God go with you," Willow replied, looking at her two servants for the last time.

Willow stopped in front of the two mares. She lovingly brought her face to each of the beautiful animals, tears flowing down her face. She patted their necks, then moved back as the soldiers moved out onto the alley. Before they were out of sight, the one called Curtis turned back to Cordelia, his lips pursing into a kiss. The finger on the trigger of the Sharps Carbine relaxed, and the three scouts followed the small assemblage into the woods beyond the alley.

That was the extent of their goodbye. Jethro and Esther led the mares down the street to the woods as the two soldiers rode behind them, their guns pointed. Willow put her arms around Cordelia, thankful the soldiers were gone. Martha, Louise, and Lewis were equally thankful they weren't made to go with the Yankees. The trio had no intention of riding off with the likes of them!

"Well, we still have some vegetables, and they didn't find the other meat we buried in the stable," Willow concluded.

The events of the afternoon had left the residents of Willow Ashby's home unsettled.

"From now on, we must bury anything of value. Cordelia, perhaps we should use the crates."

Cordelia didn't want to think about the contents in the crates. She suggested that the crates be left just as they were, as a means of deception. Perhaps they wouldn't think about looking elsewhere if the crates appeared to be more interesting.

That evening, Martha sat in the kitchen, looking at the area that was clearly Esther's domain. She wasn't a cook, but she would have to take on the job since the Yankees snatched Esther and Jethro. Cordelia stepped in, catching Martha unaware.

"I used to find that when something was bothering me, I always felt better when I sat on the bed in Mammy Cilla's cabin," Cordelia shared.

Martha smiled, remembering how she felt in the safety of her mammy and pappy's cabin back on Dr. Dryer's plantation. She remembered growing up with Pharaoh and a young Priscilla. Priscilla wasn't dark like Pharaoh; she had a lighter brown hue to her skin tone. Maybe that was what made her feel like she was special. Martha also remembered Massa Dryer and his walks down to the quarters after his young wife passed away. His clandestine visits to Celine's cabin were not lost on Martha, whose cabin was next door. A young girl herself, she felt that Massa Dryer set quite a store in Celine, and later her daughter, Priscilla.

"I 'member times back befo' I wuz given ta Miz Willow. Massa Dryer give Priscilla to his youngest, Lucretia. That be yor mama."

Cordelia missed Mammy Cilla still. She wanted to know more about her mother as well, and she didn't feel comfortable inquiring about her to Aunt Willow. She continued to listen to Martha, whom she had *taken a shine to,* as Old Thomas used to say.

"Martha, I didn't tell Aunt Willow this, but I found a paper in the crate that said Mammy Cilla was free. My Grandfather had given Mammy her freedom, but I guess Mother died before she could give the paper to her."

Martha was treading on dangerous ground discussing such things with Cordelia. She knew her mistress would reprimand her for talking about the Dryer family.

"Miz Cordelia, maybe it be for de best ef you jes' let it go."

Cordelia felt Martha knew something that she wasn't saying, but agreed for now to let it go. She was about to ask Martha if she would fix the rip in the hem of her dress when a noise out in the stable startled them. It had already gotten dark, and both women were afraid that the Yankee soldiers had come back to look for more food and valuables in the stable.

"Martha, go fetch Aunt Willow. Tell her to bring the pistol."

Martha did as she was told, quiet as a mouse. Cordelia felt as if her heart would beat through her chest, the thought of the soldiers still fresh in her mind. Ashen-faced, Willow appeared at the kitchen door. Cordelia motioned to be quiet, then stood and motioned for her aunt to give her the gun. Willow was afraid, but couldn't put her niece in harm's way.

"I'll go. You and Martha go inside and stay in the front parlor," Willow said, her voice a whisper, but with determined authority.

Before she could close the door behind her, an arm came from the darkness, putting a hand over her mouth to muffle the scream that rose from her throat.

"Shh, Mrs. Ashby. It's me, Gibson Hughes!" Gibson whispered, pulling her into the back of the house and quickly closing the door.

Clearly shaken, but thankful to have a male in the house, Willow all but collapsed onto the bench that sat beside the back door.

"Mr. Hughes, Providence has brought you to us. We just had the most terrifying encounter with the Yankee soldiers, and they took Esther and Jethro. They even took Molly and Patsy," she blurted breathlessly.

Gibson took off his hat, then pulled the drapes together at the window.

"Those soldiers won't be bothering anyone again, Mrs. Ashby. Molly and Patsy are safely returned to the stable, eating their oats," Gibson said quietly.

Willow didn't understand, but she took Gibson by the hand. Tears filled her eyes as she was relieved to have her prized gray mares back in her possession. She didn't bother to ask about Jethro or Esther.

"Mrs. Ashby, the others are waiting for me in the stable. I can't stay but a minute. I need to see Miss Cordie."

Willow stood, leading Gibson down the long hallway to the front of the house, where he saw Martha, Cordelia, Louise, and Lewis sitting quietly in the parlor. Cordelia let out a gasp when she saw Gibson standing beside her aunt. Willow placed the pistol back inside the table in the hallway.

"Gibson! Thank goodness you're here. We have been so afraid!" Cordelia said, her arms going around his neck to hug him tightly.

Gibson breathed in the scent of Cordelia, a mere memory only hours before. He wanted to talk to her in private, but knew propriety dictated that being alone with Cordelia would not be fitting or proper. Willow moved to the doorway, motioning for her servants to follow her.

"Mr. Hughes, take all the time you need. You and Cordelia may speak in private."

Willow pulled the pocket doors together, and soon her footsteps faded. Gibson pulled Cordelia close to him once again, living what he had only been able to dream before. For the first time, Cordelia didn't care about being proper. When Gibson finally released her, he held her hands in his. He marveled at her dainty fingers and soft skin. There were so many questions Cordelia had for Gibson, but she didn't want to waste a moment of their time together. It was he who spoke first.

"Cordelia, I'm going to be riding to Chattanooga tonight. I want to give you something before I leave," he said, reaching into his haversack.

He pulled out a piece of material that was rolled into a cylinder. He pulled forth a gold ring with an oval emerald in the setting. Gold filigree wrapped around the stone. Cordelia had never seen anything so beautiful. Gibson held the ring in his hand.

"This was my grandmother's wedding ring. She lived in Wales and came to the United States with my grandfather upon their marriage. It was in my mother's possession, and she gave it to me when I visited her last. I told her about you, Cordelia."

Cordelia wasn't sure what the ring meant. He hadn't even spoken to her about a future. She looked at him quizzically.

"When this war is over, I would like to make you my wife, if you would wait for me."

Cordelia couldn't believe her ears. She had never even had a suitor before. But she was smitten with Gibson Hughes. As she stood pondering such things, Gibson was nervously awaiting a reply.

"I know this is sudden, but believe me, I have thought of little else since you pulled the pistol on me in the stable," he said with a sly smile.

Cordelia smiled at the memory of their last time together. She put out her hand for Gibson to place the ring on her finger.

"Yes, Gibson. I'll wait for you. It's beautiful!" Cordelia proclaimed.

Knowing it was improper, Gibson put his hand under Cordelia's chin, lifting her face to his. His lips touched hers ever so softly, a heady sensation overtaking him. For a moment, the two stood in a long-desired embrace. Finally, it was Cordelia who moved away.

"It isn't safe here, Gibson. There are still Yankees all around the town."

"I know, but the two who accosted you are no longer a problem."

Cordelia didn't understand. She didn't realize Gibson had observed the whole scene unfold from behind the smokehouse. Another scout, positioned in the magnolia tree to the side of the house, kept his gun aimed at the Union soldiers. A third scout was hiding beneath the cover of the gazebo.

"Whatever you have done, thank you," Cordelia countered.

"I have to go now, but I'll write when I can. Tell no one that I was here. Goodbye, Cordie," Gibson said, pulling her close once more and sharing one last kiss.

Within minutes, he silently walked back into the dark of night, joining the scouts who had been hiding in the stable. Before daylight, the three would walk to their waiting horses at the undertaker's stable, where they would continue their work with Coleman's Scouts.

Summer dragged on, as did the war. Anna Mosby was dealt a double hand of fate in the death of her brother, Jed, and her fiancé, Sam Walker. She had been helping her mother, Jennie, run the family plantation since her father left to join the Confederate Army in early 1862. Now, both brothers were lying buried in local cemeteries near their final battles. Sam's body was recovered by a servant and brought back to be buried in Franklin. Cordelia and Willow, along with Lewis, Martha, and Louise, traveled to the Mosby home to attend the burial.

Willow's servants remained with her throughout the summer, toiling alongside their mistress in the constant upkeep of the grounds around the home, as well as keeping the garden tended and food on the table.

Cordelia celebrated her 21st birthday without the excitement or fanfare other birthdays with Willow had afforded her. She had made plans to travel to Nashville to claim the inheritance her father had bequeathed her upon his death, and Willow, afraid to leave her home for an extended period, requested the services of Dr. Caldwell to accompany Cordelia. He had graciously escorted Willow to Nashville when Simon was injured and furloughed to a hospital in town. Louise was sent along to attend to Cordelia. Kate Caldwell had declined the offer to come to Willow's house to spend the doctor's absence with her. Since the death of their only son, Will, Kate had found that staying near home and being around Will's things was more pleasurable to her.

In early September, Dr. Caldwell, Cordelia, and Louise boarded the train for Nashville. Upon their arrival, the small party noticed a great change in the town since their last visit. The Female Academy and the Western Military Academy were now Federal hospitals. The Union Army's presence in the subjugated town made Cordelia quite uneasy.

Wasting little time, Cordelia went to the law office of Singleton & Prewitt to discuss the matter of her father's will. A gentleman in a gray frock coat with a purple satin vest met them at the doorway.

"Good afternoon," he said to Cordelia and Dr. Caldwell.

Dr. Caldwell made their introductions, and Mr. Hiram Singleton led them into a small room. Dr. Caldwell inquired as to whom Cordelia could speak in regards to claiming the funds left in her father's will. Mr. Singleton explained that Cordelia would be given the amount of money that was placed in their care four years prior.

After Mr. Singleton had gathered the necessary information to verify Cordelia's identification, he presented her with a leather wallet. Inside were the crisp bank notes totaling the sum of two thousand dollars. Cordelia wasn't disappointed in the amount, as she expected it to be far less.

"Now, Miss Barlow, I would caution you against milling about the town with such a large sum of money. Perhaps it would be best if you allow Dr. Caldwell to secure it upon his person until you're safely home."

Cordelia took the wallet and handed it over to Dr. Caldwell. They thanked Mr. Singleton, and quietly left the office. Without harassment from Union soldiers who were about the town, they made their way to the depot and boarded the train for Columbia. It wasn't until they reached Willow Ashby's home that they could breathe a sigh of relief. Willow thanked Dr. Caldwell, inviting both him and Mrs. Caldwell for the evening meal. Eager for the company, he accepted. That evening, Cordelia shared the amount of her inheritance with Willow. She would place the money up inside the fireplace, hanging from the damper hook. She would go there as money was needed. She felt safe that the Yankee soldiers wouldn't think to look there.

Simon got a letter to his mother late in 1863. The package she had sent early in the summer had finally reached him, for which he was grateful. Since the last letter, the 1st Tennessee had seen fighting in Chickamauga, Chattanooga, and Missionary Ridge. He had formed with the rearguard, and Providence had spared him further injury. It was in the letter that arrived for Willow that Simon briefly told her of losing his best friend, Dooley Eldridge, at the battle of Stones River. He told of the morale boost to the soldiers when General Bragg was reassigned to President Davis in Richmond. A new tide had turned in the ranks, and General Joseph E. Johnston took command of the Army of Tennessee. It was during this new command that Simon would be given rations that he had all but forgotten were possible. New uniforms were given to those in need, and a furlough was granted. He wrote about taking an excursion with another private and a captain. He met a pretty young girl whom he said reminded him an awful lot of Cordie. Willow was thankful that Simon had been able to regain his health following his wounding at Murfreesboro. She would learn of a sad tale, about a young man who lived just down the road in Smyrna. Sam Davis had been part of a group of elite sharpshooters who had been working behind enemy lines. He had been captured and, refusing to give up the names of his fellow Scouts, was shot by the Yankee army. Upon hearing this, Cordelia had to wonder about Gibson's safety.

Willow decided in her own letter to explain the events of the evening that Jethro and Esther took flight with the Yankee soldiers. Keeping her word, no mention of Gibson's coming to their aid was mentioned. She wrote of town news, but even that was meager.

Another holiday season would find Willow and Cordelia making the best during wartime. Willow decided to have several of the local families to her house for a gathering. Since so many were doing without, she felt that perhaps if each person brought a dish, it would seem that they had taken part in a much bigger affair. Lewis, Louise, and Martha had risen to the occasion of preparing and serving Willow's portion of the meal. Women took to wearing their nicest evening dresses, if they were still pieced together. It was late October, and the Confederates had taken up residence in and around the city of Columbia. For the first time since the Yankees had occupied Middle Tennessee early in 1862, Cordelia felt that perhaps the war would end soon.

The families who came to dine with Willow were in various stages of mourning. The town of Columbia had given its fair share of young and promising lives. Willow had made every effort to minister to each family upon the news of their loss. Many of the servants had left with the Yankees as they moved south toward Chattanooga earlier in the year. Now, the families who lived in town had few if any servants still in their homes. Willow had opened her home to the families of Columbia, and her home on West 7th Street became a place where the names of their fallen sons and husbands were still spoken as heroes, and where a meal could be taken with this kind Southern lady at a moment's notice.

It was during the early part of 1864 that word from Gibson Hughes reached Cordelia. When she saw the postmark, her heart sank.

"Oh, no. Gibson is writing from a prison camp. Aunt Willow!" she said, her throat tightening with fear.

She read the few lines as Willow and Martha sat silent.

"He said that he was taken prisoner in Georgia, along with the two men who were with him."

Willow had heard how horrible the conditions were in the Northern prison camps. She said a quiet prayer for his safe return.

"Did he say to which prison camp he was sent?" Willow inquired.

"Yes, he says he is in prison at Point Lookout, in Maryland."

The conditions in which Gibson and the other Confederate soldiers were living were brutal, to say the least. The prison was notorious for overcrowding, and the number of prisoners sometimes reached as high as 15,000 or more. Gibson had been incarcerated for a few months, and had already experienced hunger like he had never known.

Cordelia decided to offer her services to the hospital in town. If she couldn't help Gibson and the poor soldiers at Point Lookout, perhaps she could channel her love through service to her country and those who were injured on the battlefield.

In September of 1864, she would begin a daily ride by horse and buggy to St. John's Episcopal Church, west of Columbia. The sights, sounds, and smells she encountered would remain with her for the rest of her life. The Confederate Army would soon experience unprecedented carnage at the Battle of Franklin, only two months away. The armies of the North and South would find the towns of Columbia and Franklin during the last months of 1864. The South, and Willow Ashby's family, would be forever changed.

Chapter 37

Simon Ashby, of Company H, had followed the Maury Grays from their mustering out in the spring of 1861. Wounded once, he had been patched up and sent back with his regiment. In early September, Simon and the 1st Tennessee would be part of the loss at the Battle of Atlanta. General Johnston's replacement, John Bell Hood, would march his 38,000-man army north, back to the land Simon longed to see.

General Nathan Bedford Forrest's cavalry, going ahead of Hood's army, crossed the Tennessee River at Florence, Alabama, on the 21st of November. The general's main objective was to head for Columbia on the Duck River. This was the direct line to Nashville. Union General John Schofield and his 30,000 troops were also headed to Columbia. In a short amount of time, General Hood would slip around General Schofield's flank, obstructing his path at Spring Hill.

Early in the day on November 24, General Schofield began his march north to Columbia. Cordelia had risen early that morning. The sound of the Union Army coming into Columbia caused the residents to close their shutters and huddle together in their parlors. Willow had been observing the soldiers from the third floor of her home. She pulled her shawl around her neck, trying to ward off the chill that seemed to be coming from within. The Athenaeum Girls School was visible from her perch, and it was here that General Schofield had made his headquarters. The thought of the Yankees camped in and around this place of learning and culture made Willow shudder.

Cordelia went into the parlor, where Martha, Louise, and Lewis were busy closing and latching the rest of the lower floor shutters. The day was already dreary; closing the shutters and not lighting the lamps made it even more so.

"Lewis, do not open the door for anyone, do you hear me?" Cordelia instructed.

Cordelia went to the mantel and lit a single candle. Knowing everyone's nerves were already frayed, she asked that Louise and Martha commence working on the mending. The blockade had been successful in halting the bolts of material that Willow had grown accustomed to purchasing. Louise had taken to turning Willow's lovely day dresses inside out, and Cordelia was given to wearing simple cotton day dresses. Working at the hospital necessitated a more practical attire. Willow would not be seen, however, without her earbobs or rings.

Willow came down from her vantage point. As she rounded the landing to the stairs, a loud banging on the front door startled her.

She peeped out the small hole in the large wooden door. Standing on her porch were three Union soldiers. She took a deep breath, looked back at the scared faces in the parlor, then opened the door.

"Yes?" she said calmly to the soldiers.

The soldiers walked in, not waiting to be invited. Willow was shoved into the hall tree, momentarily losing her balance.

"You got any Negras in here?" the Captain asked.

Willow regained her composure, walking in front of the soldiers, blocking the formal parlor doorway.

"We need your Negra to help dig trenches. Is he all you got?"

Willow looked at Lewis, the faithful butler and manservant of her husband for many years. His expression was that of confusion.

"Captain, my servant is up in years. I don't think..."

The captain turned to Willow, cutting her sentence off before she could finish.

"He'll do. Come on, old man. You are conscripted into the Union Army," he barked.

Without another word, Lewis was led from Willow's home. Cordelia stood, afraid to move. When the door closed, Willow did something that had become a ritual ~ she locked the door.

"Cordelia, we are almost out of wood. Lewis went to the sawmill earlier this week, but I don't know if we will have enough to last through next week."

"Aunt Willow, what will become of Lewis?" Cordelia asked.

Willow had already lost Cyrus, Esther, and Jethro to the Yankees. Now she had lost the only male on the premises. She was especially saddened by the Yankees taking Lewis. He had been with her husband since before she and Elijah married.

"I don't know, dear. He is not a fieldhand. The Yankees won't care."

The following day, November 25th, the Army of Tennessee reached the fortifications south of town. The townspeople heard the artillery in the distance, and many took to their cellars, afraid the Yankees would commence firing in the streets. Simon and the Maury Grays had left the city four years earlier with 120 men eager to whip the Yankees. Company H would have only 12 of those original men that day as they marched past Columbia and on to Spring Hill.

Martha and Louise took the shovel and went about digging up the ham that had been buried sometime earlier. Willow felt that the armies would not have time to forage for food with a battle so close, perhaps giving her household the opportunity to have a more satisfying meal. While Martha and Louise prepared supper, Willow and Cordelia sat near the fireplace in the formal parlor. It had become necessary to use only what rooms were essential. They also had taken to sleeping on large pallets on the floor, staying downstairs except to perform their daily toiletries.

When Hood's Army of Tennessee reached Spring Hill, the Yankee army had made a mad dash towards Franklin. Pieces of artillery, knapsacks, guns, and abandoned wagons were scattered along the turnpike in their haste to retreat. That evening, the fires still burned around Columbia, a farewell from the Union soldiers. Cordelia and Willow spent this night unaware how close Simon had been, marching nearby and crossing the Harpeth River. In a matter of days, the South's gallant and brave would lie strewn across every field and road in Franklin.

Chapter 38

The 1st Tennessee followed General Hood and the Army of Tennessee up the Columbia Pike into Franklin. Simon had worn the shoe leather completely off the soles of his shoes when the Army of Tennessee marched out of Chattanooga. After the Battle of Kennesaw Mountain, he lifted a pair of boots from a dead Yankee sergeant, who was obviously no longer in need of the finer things in the war. Unfortunately, others had been barefoot or nearly so, and now, in the cold of winter, had taken to wrapping strips of blanket or bandages around their cracked and bleeding feet.

On the morning of November 30th, Martha and Louise were sent to the chicken coop to gather what eggs there were to be found. It seemed even the two chickens had become downtrodden with the Yankees being so close. Thankfully, the Yankees hadn't found them, as Martha had stuffed them into an old feed sack and hidden them inside Willow's grandfather clock. How the two Yankee soldiers failed to hear the clucking was beyond her.

On this morning, Jennie Mosby and her daughter, Anna, carried wood in from the pile that hadn't been depleted by the Union soldiers. The Yankees had camped in their backyard before moving on to get into position for the upcoming battle. After cleaning out the smokehouse and cellar, only a small amount of food remained hidden under the floorboard in the kitchen. Bess watched the horses thundering past the house, and came up from the barn.

The residents of Franklin soon became part of the battle. Jennie pulled the shades and shutters, naively thinking this would be of some kind of protection. Anna, still in mourning from her fiancé's death, would be appropriately dressed for the carnage that was still to come.

Simon marched on the double quick, feeling he was ready to face whatever fate the good Lord had in store for him. He had seen most of his regiment cut down like a farmer takes a scythe to wheat. He was wearing the pistols that his father had carried to Vera Cruz, and had his Enfield rifle and bayonet at the ready.

When the 1st Tennessee reached the southern edge of town, the Union army was waiting behind their fortifications. The fighting had already begun and, for a moment, Simon wanted to run the opposite direction. When he turned to see what lay behind him, he couldn't have run if his legs would have carried him. Behind him were the bravest of the brave, those soldiers from the 1st Tennessee who had been at Lookout Mountain, marched from Mississippi through the hottest of days, often without a drop of water on their parched tongues. No, Simon couldn't have left these valiant warriors to fight the invaders without him. He turned, pulled out his father's pistols, and moved forward behind his corporal.

Anna sat beside her mother in the cold cellar, feeling the earthen structure shake from the vibrations of cannon fire. Bess sat trembling with each quake. For three hours, the frightened trio sat shivering in their underground cloak of protection. Prayers were said for the soldiers fighting on the land around them, for the protection of the people who lived in the line of battle; all were remembered as the petitions went up in a sorrowful litany.

Simon moved over the dead and dying as if he were hovering above the scene. He heard the screams, saw the unbelievable storm of bullets exploding into the men to his left and right. He moved toward the Union line where they were entrenched behind their breastworks. Simon couldn't believe the carnage that lay before him, generals lying dead upon their lifeless steeds, swords still gripped in their outstretched hands. Even death, the final act on the battlefield, was eerily suspended in time. The sight of General Cleburne riddled with bullets caused Simon to pause and say a silent prayer for this good and gallant soldier.

Passing over the trench, Simon saw soldiers lying one atop the other, like toys thrown down by a child now tired of the game of war. As the weary group moved on, they continued firing, with the smoke and fire around them rising to heights far above their heads. In the confusion, Simon lost sight of his regiment. He felt his feet hit the head of a poor soldier who no longer felt the pain of his wound. As he continued on, the whirring Yankee bullets continued to hit the living and the dead. Finally, passing onto a portion of the battlefield that was lit by fire, Simon saw he was now in the rear of his skirmish line. He could see the color bearer leading the way up the street into town. Soldiers from both sides were firing across the street and from behind houses, no longer in lines of battle. It was here that he faced a Union private from Ohio. Both drew, both fired. Simon's shot landed squarely in the throat of the Ohio private. Blood gushed from the wound, leaving the soldier's head flopped over on his shoulder in a hideous position. As the soldier collapsed to the ground, Simon screamed out in pain from the blast that tore a hole into his side. As he fell, there on the ground was the flag of his regiment, stained with the blood of not only the fallen Yankee soldier lying beside it, but now his own.

For the next two hours, the Angel of Death would collect a bounty of souls. Over 2,000 would die on this day; another 6,500 would lay wounded. Countless others would remain missing. The wounded Confederates would be taken to one of 44 buildings designated as field hospitals. The home of the McGavock's, Carnton Plantation, would also see hundreds of soldiers brought into the house, as well as occupying every square inch of the property. Six Confederate Generals would be brought to the porch of the home, where bereaved soldiers filed past.

Simon lay among the dead and dying. Throughout the night, he drifted in and out of consciousness. Prayers from the dying lifted into the air as many petitioned for their souls to be welcomed into Heaven. Others called out for wives and sweethearts, while most just called out for their mothers. It was a pitiful sight. Simon thought of his mother, and how sad he would be to not have her tend him back to health. Another face entered his abysmal sleep. It was that of a young woman, dark haired and quite lovely. She smiled at Simon, holding out her hand to him, beckoning him to get up, come to her. Trying to rise from his prostrate position, he fell back to his spot on the cold ground, next to the Union soldier whom he had killed.

Chapter 39

News of the carnage in Franklin quickly reached the town of Columbia. The casualty lists would soon make the newspapers, but for now, Willow and Cordelia waited for any news that could be given. Dr. Caldwell felt he could be most useful making his way to the battle site. He went early the following morning, taking with him Fred Hatcher, a young man who had moved into the doctor's home and was studying to become a doctor. Since the occupation two years prior, Fred had left the University in Nashville and come to work under Dr. Caldwell.

As the doctor and his apprentice made their way into the town, soldiers were already on burial detail for the Confederate dead. The dead lay everywhere. Townspeople had begun coming out of their cellars, looking at the massacre that had happened the night before. Their homes were now riddled with bullets from both Union and Confederate guns.

Dr. Caldwell offered his services, and those of Fred Hatcher, at a home near the McGavock's cotton gin. The owners had fled prior to the battle, so the Confederate Army made this home one of the first field hospitals. For several hours, Dr. Caldwell helped mostly with amputations and sutures. His lack of experience in amputations didn't allow him to perform this procedure alone. Thankful for that, he and Fred worked as needed, praying they could get word about several of the boys from Maury County. He knew that Simon Ashby had come to Franklin, but he wasn't sure of Company H's status.

Early on the morning of December 1, Anna Mosby opened the door to a ragged soldier. He was a surgeon with the 47th Tennessee, asking for the use of their home. There were soldiers in wagons and some were being carried on the backs of other soldiers. She opened the door, allowing the young doctor access to the spacious home. He gave instructions quickly, and the women in the house began to move the smaller pieces of furniture out of the way, while several soldiers began taking the larger tables and moving them to the rooms with the most light. Soldiers began carrying the wounded into the bedrooms, their blood staining the carpets and polished wood floors. Bess carried countless buckets of water from the well, while Jennie and Anna carried what sheets and pillowcases they could find to be used for the soldiers. Many would be torn into strips for bandages. This would be one of the busiest hospitals east of town. Soldiers were still being removed from the battlefield, wounded and clinging to life. One of those poor souls was Simon Ashby.

What brought Dr. Caldwell to Franklin would be called divine intervention by some. As he worked straight through the day, only breaking to choose which soldier he would operate on next, he was sent outdoors in the cold to see which of the wounded in the yard needed immediate attention.

As he moved through the piteous site, a familiar face gazed up with glassy eyes from his spot under the dying tree. Dr. Caldwell immediately bent down to Simon and saw that he had received a gut shot, inevitably a mortal wound. His heart broke seeing the young man, a childhood friend of his own now-deceased son, Will.

"Son, do you know who I am?" Dr. Caldwell asked, bending down to hear the dying boy's reply.

"Yes sir, I know. Am I dying, Doctor Caldwell?" Simon asked, his voice barely audible.

Dr. Caldwell yelled for a soldier to get a litter, so that he could bring Simon into the house. When the litter bearer saw the wound in Simon's side, he proclaimed without feeling, "Ain't no need to bring him, Doc. He's almost gone."

The soldier, still in shock from the massacre in which he had just taken part, had become callous in his job of assessing the wounded. Not wanting to waste time on arguing, Doctor Caldwell sat on the cold ground, taking off his coat and laying it across Simon.

"Simon, is there anything you want to tell me, for your mother?" he asked, knowing Simon would soon be gone.

Simon's ashen face took on a more serene expression, resigned to his fate. He spoke in a mere whisper. "Tell Mother I love her, and Cordie. Don't leave me here. I want to be next to Father."

Before Dr. Caldwell could reply, Simon surrendered his spirit.

A soldier came to the door, yelling for the doctor to come back into the house. Dr. Caldwell asked for Simon's remains to be taken back to his home in Columbia. He directed a slave who was sitting under the tree beside his master to help him get Simon into the wagon, and summoned Fred Hatcher, who was finishing surgery to remove a minié ball from a wounded soldier's knee.

"I have to take a body back to Columbia, Fred. If you wish to remain, I will come back for you. I owe this boy his last request," he said, determined to leave.

Fred Hatcher remained that day with the wounded and dying soldiers, and would stay in Franklin for months, caring for the wounded.

As Dr. Caldwell left Franklin and moved south toward Columbia, he couldn't help but weep openly for the scores of dead being hastily interred where they fell. Fence posts, planks of wood, and anything else that could be found were the headstones for the fallen. The task that remained before him would be even more heartrending.

Chapter 40

Willow and Cordelia were in the kitchen with Martha and Louise, trying to keep busy. On this day, December 2, the newspaper would have a more detailed count of the wounded and dead from the battle in Franklin.

Cordelia put on her hat and coat, took her small coin purse from the hall table, and walked to the newspaper office three blocks into town. Several residents of Columbia were gathered, reading the list that had been published earlier that day. Looking over the shoulder of a small woman, she scanned the list of names. She read the list down to Maury County, Company H. It was there she saw Simon's name. *Ashby, Simon. Company H, 1st Tennessee. Wounded.* She felt her knees buckle, then felt the wave of nausea that accompanied the feeling of panic. *Wounded...what if he had to have his arm amputated, or perhaps he suffered a leg wound. How am I going to share this dreadful news with Aunt Willow?*

Cordelia was too preoccupied with the news of Simon being wounded to notice the wagon of Dr. Caldwell pulling in front of the town's undertaker. He walked inside, and soon after, he and the undertaker emerged. The blanket was pulled back, and Emmitt Goodson beheld the remains of young Simon Ashby. He put the blanket back in place, then he and Dr. Caldwell carried the shrouded body into his establishment.

Inside the formal parlor, Willow sat writing her weekly correspondences. Even during the last months when writing paper had gotten harder to come by, Willow continued to send condolences to the families who were grieving the loss of family members. She heard the front door close, but didn't look up from her task. Cordelia came into the parlor and sat down on the velvet settee. She wasn't sure how to tell her Aunt Willow what she had seen on the casualty list.

"Aunt Willow, I saw a paper today. I need to speak to you about it."

Willow turned from her writing. Before she could answer Cordelia, the front bell rang.

"Martha, please answer the door," Willow called.

Martha came from the dining room, where she had been setting the table for dinner. She peeked out the side window. Seeing it was Dr. and Mrs. Caldwell, she opened the door.

"Afternoon, Dr. Caldwell, Miz Kate," Martha said.

Dr. Caldwell still had blood on his coat, and this didn't escape the all-seeing eyes of Martha. Her gaze was broken when the doctor spoke.

"Martha, is Mrs. Ashby in? I would like to speak to her."

Martha moved to allow Dr. Caldwell and his wife's entry into the house. She led them into the parlor where Willow and Cordelia were seated. Kate Caldwell was Willow's dearest friend, and her expression told Willow that this wasn't a social call.

"Good afternoon, Dr. Caldwell. So nice of you to come, Kate. I didn't expect to see you back from Franklin so soon," she commented, a nervous tenor in her voice.

Kate sat beside Willow, with Dr. Caldwell sitting in the chair beside them. Cordelia expected that Dr. Caldwell had learned about Simon's injury and had come to tell them where they could go to see him.

"Miss Willow, I arrived day before yesterday to tend the wounded, but there were just so many. I had been doing operations through the night, but early in the morning I went out into the yard to find more men to bring into the house."

Willow began to twist her handkerchief into a knot, her eyes darting from her friend to the doctor. Swallowing the lump that had risen in his throat, he continued. "When I walked from the porch, I saw Simon lying on the ground among the injured."

Willow's gasp echoed throughout the house. Tears filled her eyes as she listened to Dr. Caldwell's account.

"Miss Willow, he had been shot in the side. There was nothing that could be done..." Dr. Caldwell's voice broke, and Kate began to sob.

The words cut through Willow's heart. Cordelia wasn't prepared for the news, even though she had just read of his wounding. She quickly went to kneel down before her aunt, to try and comfort her. The words had not yet been spoken, but Willow knew her son was gone.

"Oh Simon," she sobbed. "Please, tell me everything. I must know."

Dr. Caldwell tried to recount Simon's final moments. He brought with him a sack containing Simon's haversack, canteen, and other items he had carried with him. He brought forth the pistols that were given to him that day when he left Columbia, so proud and ready to defend his homeland. Willow sat, disbelieving. It was then that Dr. Caldwell handed her something small that was cradled in his hand.

"Miss Willow, this was on him when he passed."

Willow took the small gold chain and cross that had been her mother's. She began to weep, bringing Martha and Louise into the room. Upon seeing Simon's belongings and the gold chain, they began to wail a mournful cry. The pain overtook Cordelia, and the bright light that was Simon Ashby was forever extinguished.

Dr. Caldwell explained that he accompanied Simon's body back to Columbia, where he was at the undertaker's parlor. Martha chose Simon's cadet uniform to take for his funeral clothing. The grieving mother, sister, and servants made their way to the undertaker to see Simon.

Due to the lack of dye, traditional mourning customs were becoming harder to observe. Willow and Cordelia came back to the house and began the somber ritual of preparing their home for a funeral. Willow somehow found the strength to write the announcement to friends of his passing, and neighbors and friends from the town began their visits of condolence as the casket was now brought to the home for the wake. Dr. Caldwell offered to sit with Simon's body while it remained in the parlor before burial.

Martha and Louise began making a meal with what little food there was. All of their meat, save a few bags of salt pork, was still buried under the stable floor. Black-eyed peas would also be prepared. Other food was brought to the house, but it was a time when all food items were in short supply. The outpouring of love towards Willow Ashby was evident in the citizens' offerings to the grieving mother.

Cordelia had written to Gibson that evening, describing the funeral services of her cousin. She would tell Gibson everything someday. For now, she longed to have him with her. She seemed to have lost Simon before she could even get to know him. Now, she wasn't even sure that Gibson was among the living. Exhausted from the sadness of the day, she collapsed onto her bed, the cold quilt taking her breath as she lay upon it. As she cried herself to sleep, a soothing voice soon filled her ears. She heard the soft, melodic voices of Mammy Cilla and Nancy. She heard the slave songs that were so comforting to her as a child. It was Mammy Cilla who comforted Cordelia once again, even if it was only in her dreams.

The Battle of Nashville quickly followed the Franklin battle. From there, the Confederate Army would see its fight become a *Lost Cause.* Willow and Cordelia tried to find comfort in one another's company. Christmas wasn't celebrated that year at Willow's home. Spring came, and Lewis found his way back to Willow's home. He had run away from the Union as they were heading south. He showed up one afternoon, quite ragged and nearly a skeleton. Asking no questions, Willow welcomed her faithful servant home. He cried when he saw the mourning drapes still about the house. He loved Simon, and grieved along with Martha and Louise.

News of the war's end came that April. The town of Columbia read of the surrender as did the rest of the South. Cordelia received word that all prisoners of war would be released. Soon, soldiers would start for home. The war had taken the most promising, the lifeblood of the South. Now, the wounded and maimed would begin marching home to a Southland that had been laid to waste.

The country soon would be in mourning again, this time for the President of the United States. Cordelia and Willow read the account of how John Wilkes Booth killed President Lincoln at Ford's Theater. There had been enough killing. The nation read the account of the conspirators, onc of whom was a lady, being rounded up and hanged. Willow felt sorrow for this woman, her life ending in such a horrible way. Somehow, she felt, the country must come together now. She and Cordelia prayed nightly for Gibson. The two continued their weekly trip to Rose Hill Cemetery to tend to Simon's grave.

On July 7, a train bringing soldiers into the depot sounded its whistle as it pulled to a stop. Cordelia had been sitting on the porch of her aunt's home, as the heat had become almost unbearable inside the house. She caught sight of Gibson Hughes as he made his way up the street with the help of another. Throwing down her fan, she leapt from porch, not caring about her underskirts showing as she darted towards the feeble soldier.

"Gibson! I've missed you so!" she said, wrapping her arms around him and kissing his cheek.

The soldier pulled her back, as if Gibson were a leper.

"Miss, you might want to wait before you hug him. He's crawling with graybacks."

Gibson smiled warily, his face covered with whiskers, his eyes sunken into their sockets. If Cordelia hadn't been so jubilant to see him, she might have thought him a ghost. Her love for Gibson masked the obvious stench and filth from her senses. It had been two years since she saw him last, and even though he was emaciated, he still was here, alive! Doing as she was told, she pulled back. She walked alongside him, helping him up the steps and into the house.

"Aunt Willow! Gibson's home!" she excitedly announced, as they made their way into the house.

"Miss Cordie, I should go out to the stable. Have Martha fetch me a boiling pot. I'll clean up there," Gibson said, his voice but a whisper.

Willow saw how filthy Gibson was, and put the women to work getting water ready for his bath. Lewis helped undress him and burn the rags he was wearing. His hat and coat were put in a sack; he didn't want to part with them.

After he had been scrubbed and shaven, what food they had was prepared for Gibson's homecoming. It would be two days before Cordelia could speak to him, as he slept soundly in the room that was once Simon's. There would time for him to learn about Simon's death, and Cordelia would learn about his involvement with Coleman's Scouts. By Christmas of 1865, the two would be married at St. Peter's Episcopal Church.

Anna Mosby and her mother, Jennie, arrived for the nuptials. Evan Mosby had been wounded at the Battle of Franklin, and had been within a mile of the house when he was struck. He lost his leg, but survived. He was slowly recuperating at their home and would be unable to attend. Anna would be Cordelia's maid of honor, and Dr. Caldwell would stand beside Gibson Hughes. The promise between Gibson and Cordelia had been kept, and Willow's house would once again be opened up to the community. The war had taken much from them, but love remained a constant in Willow Ashby's home.

COLUMBIA, TENNESSEE, SEPTEMBER, 1872

Cordie Hughes sat rocking on the front porch, awaiting the arrival of Gibson's mother. Her young son, Simon, lay on his belly, playing with blocks on the cool stone floor of the porch. She would deliver another child later in the autumn months, which caused her to be fatigued by the sweltering heat.

Earlier in the year, Willow Ashby had suffered a stroke. She lingered a few days, smiling at her niece, but never speaking again. Cordelia stayed by her side, Martha tending to young Simon. Upon her passing, the town of Columbia would give her a fitting tribute to honor her kind, Christian character and giving spirit. Dozens gathered at her gravesite in Rose Hill Cemetery, next to her husband and son. Her passing left the large house on West 7th Street to Cordelia and Gibson. It was far too large for them alone, so Gibson had sent for his mother to come from Goodlettsville to live with them. She would be able to help Cordelia with the arrival of their second child.

Gibson had taken the law books that Absalom Barlow had left to him and opened up a small office in the rear of the home. During Reconstruction, the citizens of the South saw many changes in their cities, with the freed slaves trying to make a life for themselves in an impoverished state. Gibson Hughes was known in town for helping whomever needed legal advice or help dealing with the Yankee carpetbaggers who had found their way into the town.

Cordelia couldn't have known what the future would hold for her as she stood at the front door, knees shaking, that spring day in 1860. She couldn't have known what family secrets would be revealed once she met the name on the yellowed piece of paper from so long ago.

She was thinking about that first summer at Willow Ashby's home when a wagon being pulled by a pair of mules caught her attention in front of the house. The driver, a middle-aged Negro, sat beside a younger woman with a brightly colored kerchief wrapped around her head. Cordelia watched as the wagon stopped directly in front of her house. Seeing that they looked lost, she stood from her rocking chair. Simon was engrossed in his toys, so she walked down to the bottom step of the porch.

"May I help you?" she inquired of the man.

He took off his hat, which appeared to be a Union kepi. Cordelia tried to not let that interfere with her thoughts of helping the vagabonds.

"Yas'm. We's lookin' fo' Miz Willow Ashby," he said.

The woman looked up now, making eye contact with Cordelia. It was then that Cordelia made her way from the steps to the wagon.

"I'm sorry, but Mrs. Ashby passed away earlier in the year. What business did my aunt have with you? Perhaps I could help you," Cordelia kindly offered.

It was then that another woman, much older, sitting behind the driver, removed the bonnet that had covered her face from view. She stood, grabbing on to Tillie, her daughter, for support.

"Miz Cordie? Praise be, chile, is that you?" the old woman exclaimed.

Cordelia had thought she would never hear that voice again. The emotion of seeing Mammy Cilla all but overtook her, and she was barely able to speak.

"Mammy Cilla? Oh, here, let me help you," Cordelia said, half sobbing, half speaking.

Tillie and her husband got down from the wagon, helping Mammy Cilla from the box where she had been sitting. Cordelia embraced Mammy Cilla, breathing in the scent she had so often longed for.

"Mammy Cilla, I never thought I would see you again!" Cordelia said, kissing her cheek.

"Lamb, I know'd Miz Willow name from slave times, and I want to see how the baby was."

She hugged Tillie, her childhood friend. Then she remembered herself.

"Please, all of you, come into the house. I want you to meet my son and husband. There is much we have to talk about, Mammy."

Mammy Cilla and her family were welcomed into Cordelia and Gibson's home. Martha and Mammy Cilla, not having seen one another since their days on Dr. Dryer's plantation, embraced and discussed their time as slaves for the Dryer family. Cordelia would learn about Pharaoh and Silas being taken by the Union soldiers to dig trenches, and how they were both killed during the fighting near Chattanooga, where they lived. Sadly, Tillie and Mammy Cilla were all that was left of Judge Barlow's servants. Now free, they weren't bound by chains to this family, but through the love of its women, Willow and Cordelia. Cordelia would never know the bond that drew Mammy Cilla to Cordelia was more than loyalty to her family. They shared the same blood. It was Cordelia's grandfather who freed his child, Priscilla, upon his deathbed. The papers were still lying in the crate inside the barn. It was love that made her promise to protect Cordelia after her mother's death.

Cordelia offered the carriage house to Mammy Cilla and her family until they were able to find a more permanent home. As she walked Mammy Cilla to her room for the night, she kissed her withered face and told her that she loved her best.

LORI ROBERTS

Lori Roberts is an educator, historian, and presenter for historical events and workshops. The War Between the States is a particular passion of Lori's. Lori teaches United States History at the middle school level. She and her husband, Doug, have three children and three grandchildren. They live in rural southern Indiana with their golden retrievers, Gracie and Maggie, and their cat, Jackson.

CPSIA information can be obtained at www.ICGtesting.com
Printed in the USA
LVOW10s0958150713

342868LV00003B/9/P

9 780989 481496